PUFFIN BOOKS

ADVENTURES OF TIM RABBIT

'Are ye any relation of Tim Rabbit?' asked the gardener, when he caught Tim among the lettuces.

'I *am* Tim Rabbit, sir,' said Tim Rabbit quickly, and he jumped out of the man's pocket and scuttered away over the garden. 'Can't stop!' he cried, squeezing under the gate. 'I shall be late for my party!' and the gardener laughed and threw him a lettuce over the wall.

Tim Rabbit's adventures always turned out like that, because Tim was No Ordinary Rabbit, as the Fairy Queen said when he strayed by chance into her forbidden garden. Indeed, his great grandmother had saved her once when she had been in difficulties, and in return she had been watching over Tim ever since he was born to see he came to no harm. He might be caught in a poacher's net, or tricked by his enemy the Fox or the bad Magpie, but little Tim Rabbit would always have all the friends he had won by his kind deeds to help him, and a kind mother and a warm bed to return to when the day's frolics and adventurings were done.

Alison Uttley's special gift for weaving charming stories tinged with deep and subtle magic, about the lives of little farm and woodland creatures, is shown yet again in her creation of little Tim Rabbit and his friends, the Bat, Old Hedgehog, Scarecrow, Mole and Mouse. We are delighted that Tim has joined those other favourite Uttley characters, Sam Pig and Little Red Fox, which are published in Young Puffin editions.

D1379976

Alison Uttley

Adventures of
Tim Rabbit

Illustrated by A. E. Kennedy

Puffin Books
in association with Faber & Faber

Puffin Books, Penguin Books Ltd, Harmondsworth, Middlesex, England
Penguin Books, 40 West 23rd Street, New York, New York 10010, U.S.A.
Penguin Books Australia Ltd, Ringwood, Victoria, Australia
Penguin Books Canada Ltd, 2801 John Street, Markham, Ontario, Canada L3R 1B4
Penguin Books (N.Z.) Ltd, 182–190 Wairau Road, Auckland 10, New Zealand

First published by Faber & Faber Ltd 1945
Published in Puffin Books 1978
Reprinted 1978 (twice), 1980, 1981, 1982, 1984

Made and printed in Great Britain by
Hazell Watson & Viney Limited,
Member of the BPCC Group,
Aylesbury, Bucks
Set in Linotype Baskerville

Contents

I. The Riddle-me-ree

> In marble walls as white as milk,
> Lined with a skin as soft as silk,
> Within a fountain crystal clear,
> A golden apple doth appear.
> No doors there are to this strong-hold,
> Yet thieves break in and steal the gold.

Little Tim Rabbit asked this riddle when he came home from school one day.

Mrs Rabbit stood with her paws on her hips, admiring her young son's cleverness.

'It's a fine piece of poetry,' said she.

'It's a riddle,' said Tim. 'It's a riddle-me-ree. Do you know the answer, Mother?'

'No, Tim.' Mrs Rabbit shook her head. 'I'm not good at riddles. We'll ask your Father when he comes home. I can hear him stamping his foot outside. He knows everything, does Father.'

Mr Rabbit came bustling in. He flung down his bag of green food, mopped his forehead, and gave a deep sigh.

'There! I've collected enough for a family of elephants. I got lettuces, carrots, wild thyme, primrose leaves and tender shoots. I hope you'll make a good salad, Mother.'

'Can you guess a riddle?' asked Tim.

'I hope so, my son. I used to be very good at riddles. What is a Welsh Rabbit? Cheese! Ha ha!'

'Say it again, Tim,' urged Mrs Rabbit. 'It's such a good piece of poetry, and all.'

So Tim Rabbit stood up, put his hands behind his back, tilted his little nose and stared at the ceiling. Then in a high squeak he recited his new riddle:

> 'In marble walls as white as milk,
> Lined with a skin as soft as silk,
> Within a fountain crystal clear,
> A golden apple doth appear.
> No doors there are to this strong-hold,
> Yet thieves break in and steal the gold.'

Father Rabbit scratched his head, and frowned.

'Marble walls,' said he. 'Hum! Ha! That's a palace. A golden apple. No doors. I can't guess it. Who asked it, Tim?'

'Old Jonathan asked us at school today. He said anyone who could guess it should have a prize. We can hunt and we can holler, we can ask and beg, but we must give him the answer by tomorrow.'

'I'll have a good think, my son,' said Mr Rabbit. 'We mustn't be beaten by a riddle.'

All over the common Father Rabbits were saying, 'I'll have a good think,' but not one Father knew the answer, and all the small bunnies were trying to guess.

Tim Rabbit met Old Man Hedgehog down the lane. The old fellow was carrying a basket of crab-apples for his youngest daughter. On his head he wore a round hat made from a cabbage leaf. Old Man Hedgehog was rather deaf, and Tim had to shout.

'Old Man Hedgehog. Can you guess a riddle?' shouted Tim.

'Eh?' The Hedgehog put his hand up to his ear. 'Eh?'

'A riddle!' cried Tim.

'Aye. I knows a riddle,' said Old Hedgehog. He put down his basket and lighted his pipe. 'Why does a Hedgehog cross a road? Eh? Why, for to get to t'other side.' Old Hedgehog laughed wheezily.

'Do you know this one?' shouted Tim.

'Which one? Eh?'

'In marble walls as white as milk,' said Tim, loudly.

'I could do with a drop of milk,' said Hedgehog.

'Lined with a skin as soft as silk,' shouted Tim.

'Nay, my skin isn't like silk. It's prickly, is a Hedgehog's skin,' said the Old Hedgehog.

'Within a fountain crystal clear,' yelled Tim.

'Yes. I knows it. Down the field. There's a spring of water, clear as crystal. Yes, that's it,' cried Old Hedgehog, leaping about in excitement. 'That's the answer, a spring.'

'A golden apple doth appear,' said Tim, doggedly.

'A gowd apple? Where? Where?' asked Old Hedgehog, grabbing Tim's arm.

'No doors there are to this strong-hold,' said Tim, and now his voice was getting hoarse.

'No doors? How do you get in?' cried the Hedgehog.

'Yet thieves break in and steal the gold.' Tim's throat was sore with shouting. He panted with relief.

'Thieves? That's the Fox again. Yes. That's the answer.'

'No. It isn't the answer,' said Tim, patiently.

'I can't guess a riddle like that. Too long. No sense in it,' said Old Man Hedgehog at last. 'I can't guess 'un. Now here's a riddle for you. It's my own, as one might say. My own!'

'What riddle is that?' asked Tim.

'Needles and Pins, Needles and Pins,
When Hedgehog marries his trouble begins.'

'What's the answer? I give it up,' said Tim.

'Why, Hedgehog. Needles and Pins, that's me.' Old Man Hedgehog threw back his head and stamped his feet and roared with laughter, and little Tim laughed too. They laughed and they laughed.

'Needles and Pins. Darning needles and hair pins,' said Old Hedgehog.

There was a rustle behind them, and they both sprang round, for Old Hedgehog could smell even if he was hard of hearing.

Out of the bushes poked a sharp nose, and a pair of bright eyes glinted through the leaves. A queer musky smell filled the air.

'I'll be moving on,' said Old Man Hedgehog. 'You'd best be getting along home too, Tim Rabbit. Your mother wants you. Good day. Good day.'

Old Hedgehog trotted away, but the Fox stepped out and spoke in a polite kind of way.

'Excuse me,' said he. 'I heard merry laughter and

Old Hedgehog trotted away

I'm feeling rather blue. I should like a good laugh. What's the joke?'

'Old Man Hedgehog said he was needles and pins,' stammered poor little Tim Rabbit, edging away.

'Yes. Darning needles and hair pins,' said the Fox. 'Why?'

'It was a riddle,' said Tim.

'What about riddles?' asked the Fox.

> 'Marble milk, skin silk.
> Fountain clear, apple appear.
> No doors. Thieves gold,'

Tim gabbled.

'Nonsense. Rubbish,' said the Fox. 'It isn't sense. I know a much better riddle.'

'What is it, sir?' asked Tim, forgetting his fright.

'Who is the fine gentleman in the red jacket who leads the hunt?' asked the Fox, with his head aside.

'I can't guess at all,' said Tim.

'A Fox. A Fox of course. He's the finest gentleman at the hunt.' He laughed so much at his own riddle that little Tim Rabbit had time to escape down the lane and to get home to his mother.

'Well, has anyone guessed the riddle?' asked Mrs Rabbit.

'Not yet, Mother, but I'm getting on,' said Tim.

Out he went again in the opposite direction and he met the Mole.

'Can you guess a riddle, Mole?' he asked.

'Of course I can,' answered the Mole. 'Here it is.

'A little black man in a hole,
Pray tell me if he is a Mole,
If he's dressed in black velvet,
He's Moldy Warp Delvet,
He's a Mole, up a pole, in a hole.'

'I didn't mean that riddle,' said Tim.

'I haven't time for anybody else's riddles,' said the Mole, and in a flurry of soil he disappeared into the earth.

'He never stopped to listen to my recitation,' said Tim sadly.

He ran on, over the fields. There were Butterflies to hear his riddle, and Bumble-bees and Frogs, but they didn't know the answer. They all had funny little riddles of their own and nobody could help Tim Rabbit. So on he went, across the wheatfield, right up to the farmyard, and he put his nose under the gate. That was as far as he dare go.

'Hallo, Tim Rabbit,' said the Cock. 'What do you want today?'

'Pray tell me the answer to a riddle,' said Tim politely. 'I've brought a pocketful of corn for a present. I gathered it in the cornfield on the way.'

The Cock called the hens to listen to Tim's riddle. They came in a crowd, clustering round the gate, chattering loudly. Tim Rabbit settled himself on a stone so that they could see him. He wasn't very big, and there were many of them, clucking and whispering and shuffling their feet and shaking their feathers.

'Silence!' cried the Cock. 'Silence for Tim Rabbit.'

'And here's a white egg to take home with you'

The Hens stopped shuffling and lifted their heads to listen.

Once more Tim recited his poem, and once more here it is:

> 'In marble walls as white as milk,
>   Lined with a skin as soft as silk,
>   Within a fountain crystal clear,
>   A golden apple doth appear.
>   No doors there are to this strong-hold,
>   Yet thieves break in and steal the gold.'

There was silence for a moment as Tim finished, and then such a rustle and murmur and tittering began, and the Hens put their little beaks together, and chortled and fluttered their wings and laughed in their sleeves.

'We know! We know!' they clucked.

'What is it?' asked Tim.

'An egg,' they all shouted together, and their voices were so shrill the farmer's wife came to the door to see what was the matter.

So Tim threw the corn among them, and thanked them for their cleverness.

'And here's a white egg to take home with you, Tim,' said the prettiest hen, and she laid an egg at Tim's feet.

How joyfully Tim ran home with the answer to the riddle! How gleefully he put the egg on the table!

'Well, have you guessed it?' asked Mrs Rabbit.

'It's there! An egg,' nodded Tim, and they all laughed and said, 'Well, I never! Well, I never thought of that!'

And the prize from Old Jonathan, when Tim gave the answer? It was a little wooden egg, painted blue, and when Tim opened it, there lay a tiny carved hen with feathers of gold.

II. Tim Rabbit finds a Garden

Little Tim Rabbit was hopping and skipping through the fields one summer's day when he came to a place he had never visited before. A high wall of rough dark stone surrounded the far field and this had kept Tim from exploring further. On this particular day he happened to push aside the ferns that grew close to the stones. He scrambled among the foxgloves and drew away the curtain of drooping ferns. There was a little doorway hidden there, screened by the leaves. It led to a passage through the wall, and the way was lined with the brightest moss and carpeted with starry flowers.

Tim Rabbit wrinkled his little nose in delight. He crept near and stared through this doorway to the land beyond. Through it he could see green bracken, a forest of feathery fronds, with countless brown hairy stalks like the trunks of little trees in some magical fairy wood.

Tim Rabbit took a hop and then turned back and waited, listening. He took another hop and a little run, and waited with ears cocked and eyes flashing quickly about him. It didn't do to run into a trap.

Then he took a third hop and a run and he scuttled through the mossy passage to the bracken wood beyond.

He looked around. 'There's no danger. This is a fine place,' said Tim to himself. 'A great forest of small green trees. If I jump very high I could see over the tree-tops.'

He gave a leap, but the bracken was thick, and he could only see the blue sky and the curling fronds. He began to run here and there, sniffing at the summer smells of moss and ferns and hot bracken, listening to the hum of the bees and the soft flicker of the butterflies' wings.

There was a tiny path like a ribbon, and he trotted along it, eager to find where it led. Soon he left the bracken behind and came to a small sunny glade. He raced up and down the short turf with little snorts of joy. It was a garden of wild flowers set in the midst of the bracken. The circular dell had walls of green around it, and inside all the flowers of summer seemed to have pushed their way. Tim had never seen such an enchanting place.

There were wild geraniums, with their curved blue petals held up to the sky, and their umbrella leaves shading smaller blossoms. There were dog daisies, taller than Tim, white as snow, and yellow spires of asphodel, and bee-orchis, and meadow-sweet. Purple vetch climbed like a ladder to the tops of the bracken. Close to the ground, under Tim's velvety feet, grew daisies with red honey-spots, and wild thyme, scented

'I always wanted a garden of my own,'
cried Tim to a robin

and sweet, eye-bright, and scarlet pimpernel. In the centre of the garden was a little nut tree, with honeysuckle and wild roses twining around it, and scarlet strawberries growing in the stones at its roots.

Tim Rabbit ate the strawberries, and nibbled some small mushrooms which grew at the garden's edge.

'I always wanted a garden of my own,' cried Tim to a robin who sat watching him with an anxious eye. 'I always wanted a garden all my own.'

'But not this one,' said the robin, and he flew away.

'Yes. I want this one. Here I can do what I like, and it's all made ready for me. No traps, or gardeners, or snares, or dogs, or foxes.'

Tim buried his nose in the fragrant wild roses, and he picked a bunch of yellow pansies for his mother. He made a daisy chain and a pansy-ball. He rolled in a bed of woodruff, and put his head on a pillow of wild thyme. The sun beat down and the smell of the crushed thyme and woodruff was like a hayfield. Tim shut his eyes and in a minute he was fast asleep.

He was awakened by small voices like insects twittering close to his ears. Something twitched his fur, something tickled his nose. He lay very still for he had learned from his mother to sham dead in times of danger. Then, as nothing happened, he opened one eye a crack. All round him were little people, leaping, skipping, dancing among the flowers. They had round faces and tiny pointed ears and glittering bright eyes and small scarlet mouths. Their clothes were many-coloured, made of silken petals and cobwebs and scraps of feathers. Their hair was gold as sunlight. Some swung in the honeysuckle streamers, some climbed the ladders of purple vetch, others leaped in the nut tree and then dropped light as thistledown upon Tim's head. Tim was delighted with such charming little folk, but he kept very still, waiting.

'Who's this sleeping in our garden?' asked one small person, and it prodded Tim with a tiny pointed shoe.

'Who's lying on my bed of woodruff?' cried another, and it shook a tiny fist at Tim.

'Who's been eating our strawberries?' cried a third.

'And nibbling the mushrooms in our enchanted ring?' asked a fourth, and it tickled Tim's nose with a straw.

Then Tim sneezed and sat up.

'Who is it? Who is it?' they called in shrill piping voices, and they all scampered across the flowers and danced round Tim.

'Who is this stranger come to our garden?' they sang.

'It's Tim Rabbit,' said Tim, bowing politely with his paw on his heart.

'Tim Rabbit! Tim! Tim!' they mocked and they jeered and they tossed their white arms and leapt in the air. Then Tim saw they had wings, transparent as those of dragon-flies, and he stretched out his paw and tried to touch them.

'You can't catch us, Tim Rabbit,' they chanted. 'You are ours now. You are ours for ever, Tim Rabbit.

You came in our garden, you stepped through our private doorway, and now you belong to us for ever.'

'For ever. For ever!' echoed the others, and they danced and leapt as wildly as autumn leaves in a gale.

'Please, are you fairies?' asked Tim, who wasn't at all frightened.

'Fairies!' they piped in their shrill thin voices. 'What do you know of fairies? There aren't any, are there? Nobody has ever seen one and gone away to tell the tale. They don't exist. No! No! No!'

'I've heard about fairies from my mother,' said Tim, slowly. 'My great-grandmother once met a fairy.'

'His great-grandmother!' they mocked.

'The fairy was fast in a spider's web, her wing was torn and my great-grandmother set her free,' added Tim.

'Great-grandmother!' jeered the little folk.

'We must keep this young romantic rabbit with his great-grandmother tales to be our fairy steed,' said one of the crowd. 'We're tired of riding on butterflies and bumble-bees. Tim Rabbit would make a good horse.'

'Oh, no,' cried Tim, hurriedly. 'I don't want to be a horse.'

'A nice furry horse, with four little feet to be shod with silver,' said another.

'A pony, a soft-skinned pony that will gallop and trot and canter,' said a third.

'I won't be a pony,' muttered Tim.

'And we will make a saddle of moleskin.'

'And a bridle of rat-skin.'

'And reins of bat's-wing leather.'

'And spurs of hedgehog quills.'

'And a whip of green rushes.'

'And he will gallop and gallop and gallop to the world's end when we all ride on his back together.'

'And he will gallop and gallop for ever.'

Then Tim Rabbit stamped his foot at them and shook his head at them.

'I won't. I jolly well won't, so there.'

'You won't?' The fairies opened wide their slanting eyes.

'You won't. You came to our garden, slept on our bed, ate our food, made yourself at home. Now you are bound to us for ever.'

Up leapt Tim Rabbit and away he rushed, but he couldn't get out of the enchanted garden. The bracken forest stretched out its ferny arms and stayed him. The air was like a wall of steel.

The fairies snatched green rushes and bracken fronds. They lashed him, and leapt upon his back as if he were a little circus horse.

Poor Tim Rabbit! He was afraid he would have to be the fairies' horse all his life. Faster and faster he ran with his ears laid back and his eyes popping in fear, but the fairies danced on his back, they clung to his hair. They twisted a rope of traveller's joy round his neck as reins and thrust it into his mouth as a bit. They snatched a leaf of wild geranium for a saddle, and dropped the blue flowers over his head as a bridle.

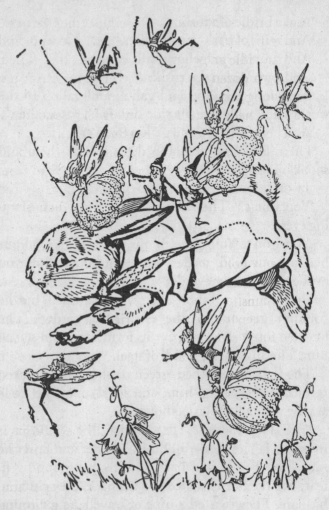

Up leapt Tim Rabbit and away he rushed

'Wear these till we've got the real leather harness,' they laughed. 'Ho, there! Ho, elves! Go and find spurs and bridle and saddle for our steed,' they called. Away flew a dozen small humble elves in brown jerkins and long brown shoes.

'Go find hedgehog quills and rat-skin and bat's-wing leather, you elves,' commanded the fairies.

Suddenly a peal of bells rang from all the harebells round about. The fairies dropped to the ground from their little horse, and Tim cowered, panting and exhausted.

'The Queen! The Queen!' cried the fairies.

Into the enchanted garden flew a fairy as lovely as a lily. A tiny gold crown rested on her hair. A sceptre of flowers was in her hand. Her dress was made of dew and sunbeams.

'The Queen! The Queen!' cried the fairies again, and they surrounded her and took her rainbow cloak and brought a blue petalled throne from the bracken for her to sit upon. She refused to sit down. She stared at Tim, and pointed her sceptre at the wretched little rabbit.

'What is all this about?' she demanded. 'Why is this animal racing up and down our private garden?'

'It's little Tim Rabbit, O Queen! We found him. We are going to keep him to be our galloping horse.'

'Our circus horse.'

'Our rocking-horse.'

'Our cart-horse.'

'Every kind of horse, even a clothes-horse.'

Fairy laughter filled the air, and then died away as the Queen stamped her foot angrily.

'No! Not Tim Rabbit! He's no ordinary rabbit! His great-grandmother was a friend of mine. She saved me once. I promised to keep an eye on all her descendants. I've been taking care of Tim ever since he was born.'

The crowd of fairies turned to Tim, and stroked his ruffled fur. They waved fans of flowers over his heated face to cool him. They gave him strawberries and honey-dew.

'Give him gifts to take home to his mother,' said the Queen. 'Then show him the way out of the garden.'

One fairy brought him a bunch of woodruff.

'This is to stuff a pillow and whoever sleeps on it will have pleasant dreams,' said she.

Another picked the blue flowers of the wild geranium.

'These blue pence will always buy things from the fairy folk. It is their money,' said she.

Another plucked a nosegay of wild thyme.

'This is to make a cup of fragrant tea,' said she.

Another gave him yellow asphodel spires.

'These will ring bells unheard by others, and make secret music for your delight.'

So every fairy gave Tim wild flowers, each of which had a magical quality.

Then they showed him the way out of the enchanted garden, through the forest of bracken to the little stone doorway in the wall.

Tim ran along the mossy passage, clutching his bouquet of flowers and herbs. When he got to the ordinary pasture at the other side of the wall he gave a sigh of relief. He turned back to draw the ferny curtain over the door, but he couldn't find the opening. The doorway had gone, the wall stood strong and sturdy, a massive pile of great blocks of sandstone, blackened and starred with lichen, rough as the farm men of two hundred years ago who made it.

Tim ran up and down, seeking the lost door, but it wasn't there. He took his nosegay home to his mother and told her the story.

'Ah yes! It's true,' said she. 'Your great-grandmother went there, and she saw the fairy Queen, whom she once helped.'

'But they nearly made me into a circus horse,' pouted Tim. 'I didn't like that at all. They beat me and lashed me and made me gallop!'

'Well, you see, Tim, you went to their garden uninvited, but your great-grandmother was a guest. There's a lot of difference when it comes to visiting the fairy folk.'

Tim and Mrs Rabbit spent the evening looking at the fairy gifts. They made the thyme tea and drank it. They listened to the music of the asphodel. They stuffed a pillow with woodruff flowers. They tossed the blue pence in the air and watched them float like

bright balloons. They bathed their eyes with eye-bright lotion, and they made necklaces with the daisies.

Although Tim went many a time to the fields, he could never again find that doorway in the wall that led to the enchanted garden of the fairies.

III. Tim Rabbit and the Bit-bat

One spring morning a black Bat came flying from her bedroom in the church roof. It was broad daylight and the sunshine made her blink and rub her eyes as she peered through the doorway. She wrapped a dark handkerchief round her head to shield her eyes from the sun's glare, and she fetched her bag from the shelf in the oak-timbered roof. Then she ventured out of doors.

She fluttered unsteadily across the churchyard and flew over the village green. The children were coming out of school, and they shouted when they saw the Bat's zig-zag flight.

> 'Bit-bat! Bit-bat!
> Catch her in your hat,'

they chanted, and they flung their hats and caps in the air and tried to catch the little creature.

'I won't be caught in your hats,' squeaked the Bat, and she dodged away with her little bag tucked under her arm.

'Fancy a dirty old woman like that coming out in

the daylight! She ought to wait till dusk,' cried the slim, neat chaffinches to the robins.

'She's not fit to be seen. Her clothes are ragged, her sleeves hang like bags, and she's as thin as a scarecrow,' chirped the sparrows. They flipped their wings in disdain and flirted their tails.

'Half-mouse, half-bird,' they whispered. 'It shouldn't be allowed.'

The Bat swept round in wide circles, so that even the swallows were amazed. She dodged between the telegraph wires, and flew through the branches of a tree, but she never touched a wire or a twig although she was so blind in the daylight.

'Old clothes! Old clothes!' mocked the starlings as they preened their glistening feathers and strutted across the grass.

'Rags and bones for sale! Rags and bones for sale!' jeered the magpies and they shook their long tails and settled on the wall to watch her.

The Bat looked in vain for a friend. Then Tim Rabbit strolled up with his paws in his pockets.

'Hallo!' cried he. 'Who is this flying about so queerly? Who is this strange creature? A winged mouse?'

'No,' squeaked the Bat in her high shrill voice. 'I'm a Bit-bat, come out early to get dinner for my children, and everyone is mocking me, Tim Rabbit.'

'Then I'll send them away,' said Tim. He rushed up and down shaking his fist at the bad little birds. Even the school children were startled when they saw Tim Rabbit's angry face and clenched fist.

'Leave that old mother Bit-bat alone.' He stamped his small foot, and glared at them. Then he scuttled away before the school children could get over their surprise.

The Bat was left in peace to fill her bag with food for her family, and she zig-zagged back to the church roof with it.

'Oh, my children!' she panted as she flew upstairs to the church rafters. 'I thought I should never get back and you would starve. If it hadn't been for a good kind rabbit I should have been driven off with never a morsel of meat for you.'

The little Bit-bats, who hung head downward in the dark corner, twittered with excitement, and swayed to and fro, as they seized the food and gobbled it up.

'A rabbit?' they cried. 'A rabbit?'

'Yes, it was little Tim Rabbit who helped me,' said their mother, as she took off her handkerchief and hung herself up by her toes at their side.

'Tim Rabbit!' they echoed. 'Tim Rabbit!'

The church rafters seemed to whisper 'Tim Rabbit,' and all the cobwebs shook like flags.

'Tim Rabbit! Do tell us about this animal! Can he fly like you? Can he hang upside down? Has he wings?' asked the little Bats.

'No, my children. He is only a small beastie, with not much sense, and no wings,' replied the mother.

'No wings,' murmured the Bats in disappointment.

'But he has a kind heart,' added the mother.

'A kind heart,' whispered the Bit-bats and they swung by their crooked toes like clever acrobats.

Down below in the church the bell-ringers came to ring for service. They pulled the red and blue striped ropes and the bells rang out high in the tower.

'Ding dong! Ding dong! Kind heart! Kind heart!'

went the bells, and the Bit-bats stretched their long ears and stopped talking. They loved the voice of the bells. It was their own music, and they thought the bell-ringers played for them alone.

'Every morning and every night we have our bells,' said the mother Bat. 'Church bells ring me to market.'

Out she flew that night in the blue dusk to finish her task. She hawked up and down, uttering shrill cries, and nobody mocked her, nobody even noticed her. The birds were already preparing for bed, and only the night moths and insects were out.

She darted over the churchyard and into the croft. She dived low and soared high. She listened to the sounds of night, the sigh of a fir-tree, the whisper of a rose-bush to its buds, the soft tinkle of a flower bell in the grass. The Bat's black bag was full and she was starting home to her hungry family when she heard another sound, a low sobbing and weeping. It came from a nettle-bed down the lane, and she threaded her way in the air above, listening with her large ears, and peering down with her dim eyes.

'I can't ever get away. I can't ever 'scape. Oh! Oh!' cried a little voice.

The Bit-bat came nearer, squeaking in her high voice, but she could see nothing except a green stretch of nettles.

'Who is it?' asked the Bat, twisting and turning and diving to the spot.

'It's little Tim Rabbit! Do you remember me? I don't suppose you do.'

'Tim Rabbit? Of course I remember you. What are you doing here? Are you lost?' asked the Bat, kindly.

'I'm caught in a net! With the meshes round my

*I'm caught in a net! With the meshes round my legs
and arms, and I can't get out'*

legs and arms, and I can't get out, and my mother will miss me. Oh dear!'

'Poor Tim Rabbit,' cried the Bit-bat, darting near. 'What can I do? How can I help you?'

'You can't,' sighed Tim. 'I must lie here till a man comes and takes me away. Oh dear! What a sad end to my young life!'

A large tear rolled down his cheek and dropped to the ground where it lay like a pearl among the nettles. The Bit-bat, too, shed a tear, but hers was a little black tear which bounced on the stones and rolled away.

'Have you any big friends who could untie the knots in the net?' asked the Bat.

'There's Johnny Scarecrow in Farmer Giles's field. He might come,' said Tim.

'The Scarecrow? A man with a face of turnip and a body of straw, isn't he?' asked the Bit-bat.

'Yes. He might come,' said Tim hopefully. 'And there's Squirrel, and Hedgehog, and Mole. They are my friends. They would rescue me if they knew about me.'

'I'll go and tell them,' said the Bat. 'Cheer up, Tim, and keep your heart beating. I won't be long.'

Away darted the Bit-bat to the Scarecrow in Farmer Giles's field, to the Squirrel in the nest in the beech-tree, to the Hedgehog trudging along the lane, to the Mole digging in the pasture, and each one promised to come and rescue Tim Rabbit.

The Scarecrow arrived first. He came striding down

the lane on his long wooden legs, with his ragged sleeve flapping and his broken hat askew over his round turnip face.

'Eh, Tim Rabbit! This is a caution and no mistake! You caught in a trap! I've been telling you about traps and such-like, and warning of you to keep away from them ever since I knowed you.'

'It's true, Johnny Scarecrow,' said Tim sadly.

'And you want me to get you out?' asked the Scarecrow, bending stiffly and examining the net.

'Yes, please,' sighed Tim.

'But I can't unfasten the knots,' said the Scarecrow. 'I haven't any fingers. Arms I've got, and a pair of old gloves but no stuffing in them.'

The Scarecrow rubbed his head with his gloves and ruffled his straw hair, trying to think of a plan to set little Tim Rabbit free.

Then the Squirrel came bounding through the trees. She stooped over Tim and tugged at the knots, but she only made them tighter.

'I can't unfasten you, Tim Rabbit,' said she, and she gaily swung her way back to home and bed.

'Ungrateful flibberty-gibbet,' snorted the Hedgehog. He struggled with the snare, but he could not unloosen the net from little Tim Rabbit.

Along came the Mole. He dug a deep hole and tried to get Tim from underneath, but the net was wound in Tim's buttons, fast in trousers and coat, tight round his fat little body, so Mole, too, had to give it up.

Poor Tim Rabbit! The Scarecrow, the Hedgehog,

the Mole stood gazing sorrowfully at their friend, and the Bit-bat flew in crooked airy paths, squeaking with anxiety at Tim's plight.

'I have a neighbour in the church tower. I'll go and fetch him,' said the Bat. She flew home and returned with a great white Owl.

'Too whit! Too whoo! Who's this? Little Tim Rabbit? I've warned you, Tim, about running wildly and never looking where you're going. Now you are caught.'

'Yes, sir. I didn't mean it. I was poking about and I got mixed up with this,' said Tim.

'Well, I can't set you free, Tim Rabbit,' said the Owl. 'However, I have a plan. Do you remember the fable of the Lion and the Mouse? Have you learned it at school, Tim?'

'No, sir. Schoolmaster didn't tell me,' said Tim.

'It's one of the stories of Old Aesop, the man who knew so much about animals. A Lion was entangled in a net and a Mouse gnawed the ropes and set him free. We will send for a Mouse, Tim.'

So everybody cheered up. The Scarecrow brushed his hair under his straw hat, the Hedgehog flattened his prickles, the Mole sleeked his black velvet coat, and the Bit-bat fastened her bonnet strings.

Off flew the Owl and he returned with a Mouse dangling in his claws.

'Save me! Save me!' wept the Mouse. 'I've done nothing amiss. Don't eat me. Not tonight.'

'Then save Tim Rabbit,' commanded the Owl.

*So the trembling little Mouse nibbled first one knot,
and then another*

'Nibble through the net and I will spare your life. For the sake of my neighbour Mrs Bit-bat, who hears the church bells with me, I will spare you.'

So the trembling little Mouse nibbled first one knot, and then another, and Tim got one leg out, and then another. All round the net went the little Mouse, biting and gnawing with its sharp teeth, and Tim pushed out his head and shoulders and waved his paws and wriggled his ears with joy as he felt the harsh net give way. The Mouse had nearly finished when footsteps came down the lane and the sound of men talking.

'I set a snare down here in the nettles,' said a voice. 'Let's see if I've caught anything.'

Then up sprang Tim, and he leapt and he slipped off his coat which was caught by a button.

A man trod heavily across the path and stooped for the net. How startled he was when a Hedgehog pricked his legs, a Mole ran over his feet, a Rabbit sprang from his hands, a great white Owl brushed his face with soft wings, a Scarecrow rapped him on the head with a wooden arm, and a Bit-bat got entangled in his mop of hair!

'Run! Run! Place is bewitched! There's Things here,' he cried, and he scampered away as fast as he could with his companion close behind him.

The Owl flew up to the church tower. The Bit-bat went to her home in the roof. The Scarecrow padded down the lane to the field. The Mouse scuttered home as fast as it could to tell how it had saved young Tim from a snare. The Hedgehog and Mole sauntered together chatting as they went along the hedge side.

Tim Rabbit hurried home to his mother who was anxiously waiting for him.

'Where have you been, Tim? It's nearly dark. I thought you were lost,' said Mrs Rabbit.

'I was caught in a net like a Lion, and a little Mouse saved me, just like Aesop's Lion,' cried Tim, flinging his arms round her.

She scolded him and kissed him.

'I expect I'm really like a Lion,' said Tim.

'You may be a Lion, I've never seen one,' said his mother. 'You are only an ordinary little rabbit to me, Tim.'

Away in the church tower the Bat was telling her children all about Tim Rabbit's rescue. They were so excited that they fell head downward into the organ loft and had to fly up again.

'Tim Rabbit!' they cried. 'What an adventure! Tim Rabbit! The bells must ring! The bells!'

And the bells sent out a merry peal which startled everyone in the village, from churchwarden to choir-boys. As for the two bad men, they are still wondering what strange fairy or pixie or gnome wore a little coat with white bone buttons which they found entwined in the fragments of the rabbit net they had set down the lane in the nettle-bed.

Mrs Rabbit started at once to make a new jacket, and this time she put brass buttons instead.

IV. Tim Rabbit and the Harvest Mouse

Tim Rabbit had a friend who lived in the wheatfield. She was the Harvest Mouse. Tim had known her for quite a long time, ever since he went out one night to find the moon, and she was kind to him. Now she was married, and she had six small children. Tim wanted to see this young family.

'I'll go and see Mrs Harvest Mouse today,' said Tim to his mother one morning. 'I want to rock the cradle, and hear the babies squeak. I want to watch the tall wheat stalks swinging in the wind. I want to hear that music the corn makes.'

'Take Mrs Mouse a little coverlet for the cradle, Tim,' said Mrs Rabbit. 'Here's one of rabbit-wool dyed with blue forget-me-nots. It will just suit them. Mrs Mouse is a nice little body, and she's not very well off. Six little children take some looking after in these days, what with owls and weasels and foxes, to say nothing of the reapers.'

She held out a little blue cot-cover, soft as down. She folded it in a neat parcel and put it in Tim's pocket.

'Give her my kind regards,' said Mrs Rabbit, and Tim nodded.

On the way across the fields he met so many rabbits, so many hedgehogs, so many Cock Robins and Jenny Wrens, as well as Peggy Whitethroat and Jenny Dishwasher, and little Sam Hare, and Moody Wap, and the Red Hen from the farm, that he quite forgot where he was going. He turned aside to play in a hollow tree, to picnic in a deserted barn, to run races round a haystack. The sun was at midday before he remembered Mrs Harvest Mouse, and away he ran to her house in the cornfield.

In the Mouse's home there had been difficulties that day. It was the worst day poor little Mrs Harvest Mouse ever remembered. This is what had happened.

An Owl came to live in the oak-tree near the cornfield, where Mrs Mouse's round straw house hung. He came there at dawn, and he decided it was as good as the church tower. There was a nice broad bough in front where he could view the land, and a shady hollow for sleeping, and a mossy doorway. He flew to the bough, stepped into the bedroom and fell fast asleep.

Deep down below in the cornfield Mrs Mouse was busy cooking the dinner. It was a special dinner, for that day the eyes of the little mice had opened, so it was a kind of birthday. The smell of the dinner roused the Owl, and he looked out from the open door high in the tree. What he saw was so interesting he blinked his eyes and stretched himself and waited.

He fixed his glowing eyes on the round cradle of straw where the six little mice wriggled. He stayed there, watching the domestic scene below. It was a charming and touching sight, he thought, and he waited like a white shadow, unseen and unheard.

Now if little Tim Rabbit had only come round the bend his sharp little eyes would have spied the Owl and he would have warned the Harvest Mouse, but Tim was far away playing in the fields.

Mrs Harvest Mouse brushed aside the leaves from her fire and opened the oven door. She lifted from the hot ashes a golden-brown macaroni cheese which had been cooking in her small leafy kitchen at the edge of the cornfield. She carried the dish carefully, wrapped in a cloth of grasses, to the stone table. Its crust was crisp as a biscuit, and the cheese was like thick cream. It was the first macaroni cheese Mrs Mouse had ever made. The farmer's wife had thrown away the cheese rinds and the macaroni was formed out of wheat ears and bits of corn stalks. There was a tiny pipkin of milk from the cow in the meadow, and an egg laid by the black hen that always lays astray. Mixed together and baked, these made a delicious dish, and Mrs Mouse was very proud of her cooking.

If only little Tim Rabbit had been there to taste it!

Mrs Harvest Mouse ran up the corn stalks and carried the six babies down to the feast. They rolled over one another in their eagerness.

'What is it? What is it?' they cried, sniffing the air.

'Macaroni cheese!' said Mrs Mouse, and they all echoed, 'Cony cheese! Cony cheese!'

They gazed about with their little bright eyes, and they squeaked for joy at the sun and the oak-tree and the waving forest of golden corn stalks. They saw the scarlet pimpernel growing like a carpet under their feet and the tiny wild pansies and the blue milkwort. The world looked very beautiful to the little mice and their mother. It looked beautiful also to the white Owl, sitting in the shadow above them.

The sunlight fell on the leafy branches, the blue sky filled the spaces. Everybody was happy, the Harvest Mouse, the six little mice, and the white Owl – and far away little Tim Rabbit was so happy he had forgotten all about them.

The Mouse tied small bibs under her children's chins, and gave each a twiggy spoon. They were a well-brought-up family of mice. They dipped their spoons in the dish on the stone table. There was no sound except the scrunch of tiny teeth and the scraping of the wooden spoons. In two minutes the dish was empty. There was not a morsel of the macaroni cheese left.

'Nice. Nice,' murmured six sleepy voices.

Mrs Harvest Mouse picked up her babies and carried them back to the hanging cradle, swinging in the corn stalks. She put them to bed just as they were, with their bibs round their necks and the wooden spoons clutched in their tight little fists. They nestled down in the soft wool with never another word, and at once they were fast asleep.

Mrs Mouse sighed with thankfulness that the meal was over. She cleared away the dirty dishes and the pipkins and the bowls and acorn-cups and she washed them in a shallow puddle in the grass. She wiped them on a towel of foxglove and hung them up in the hawthorn bush cupboard. She happened to glance towards the straw cradle. It was not there. It had completely disappeared, mice and all.

'Oh dear me! Oh dear me!' cried Mrs Harvest Mouse, and she ran in and out of the forest of corn, shaking the tall wheat stalks, pushing aside the chickweed, hunting among the scarlet and blue flowers close to the earth. She couldn't see her babies anywhere.

She ran to the hedge side, and peered into the ditch, among the meadow-sweet, but there was only a lonely Green Frog, turning somersaults all by himself.

'Oh, little Green Frog! Have you seen my cradle full of pretty pink mice?' she asked.

> 'Over he goes! Over he goes!
> Head over heels, and on to his nose,'

sang the Frog, and he turned his somersaults so quickly Mrs Mouse was quite dizzy watching him. He took no notice of her at all.

She ran across the thick grass, and lifted a dock leaf. Underneath sat a Snail, looking at himself in a drop of dew. When he saw Mrs Mouse he drew in his horns and crept back into his shell. He shut the door and glued it fast.

Mrs Mouse tapped on the striped wall.

'Oh, Snail,' she called. 'Have you seen a cradle full of pretty pink mice?'

> 'Go away, Mouse! Go away, Mouse!
> The door is shut, I'm safe in my house,'

cried the Snail. Away ran the little Mouse weeping and wailing for her lost brood.

She ran along a green lane to the gorse bush where the Hedgehog lived. She crept through a thicket of spikes. The Hedgehog was eating his dinner.

'Oh, Hedgehog!' cried Mrs Harvest Mouse. 'Have you seen a cradle full of pretty pink mice?'

> 'Needles and Pins, Needles and Pins,
> Six little mice gone Widdershins,'

said the Hedgehog, between his mouthfuls of food.

'Oh dear me!' cried Mrs Mouse. 'Nobody will talk sensibly to me. My six babies are lost on their eye-opening day.'

She left the Hedgehog, and ran along the lane. Who should she meet but little Tim Rabbit! He was hurrying along, very late for his visit.

'Oh, Tim Rabbit!' said the Harvest Mouse. 'Have you seen a cradle full of pretty pink mice?'

'No, Mrs Harvest Mouse,' said Tim. 'I was just coming to see you all. I've brought a cot-cover from my mother, and her kind regards to you.'

'Oh, Tim. The cradle has gone and all my family,' cried the little Harvest Mouse, weeping as she held the blue cot-cover.

Together they all called, 'Give her back her children, Owl'

They ran along together, back to the place where the nest had hung. Tim picked up a grey feather, soft as thistledown, which lay on the ground.

'This is the Owl's feather,' he whispered. 'There he is, up in yonder oak, sitting in the hole.'

The little Harvest Mouse ran to the foot of the tree and peered up. She spied something fluttering in the wind.

'I can see six little bibs waving up there, and the cradle is hanging by the Owl's doorway. Perhaps he hasn't eaten my family yet.'

Even as she spoke six tiny bibs came fluttering through the air like petals of plum blossom. The Mouse gathered them up and wiped her eyes upon them. She called up in her loudest, boldest squeak.

'Give me back my children, Owl.'

The Owl snored, but the Frog stopped his somersaults and hopped to the tree. The Hedgehog left his home and came there. The Snail crept out of his house and joined the company.

Together they all called, the Mouse with her squeak, the Frog with his croak, the Hedgehog with his shrill cry, and the Snail with a voice like the rustle of moss, but the loudest voice was that of little Tim Rabbit.

'Give her back her children, Owl.'

The Owl took no notice, but the little cradle rocked as the six mice leaned over to look at their mother.

'Make a nice dinner for him, and then he may leave your children,' suggested Tim Rabbit.

'There's a good smell here,' said the Hedgehog. 'Can you make another dinner like the last?'

The Harvest Mouse nodded her little head and ran back to her kitchen among the dead leaves. The others helped her.

The Hedgehog milked the cow and filled the pipkins with new milk.

The Frog collected grains of corn and straw stalks.

The Snail shook the pepper pot and sprinkled the salt.

Tim Rabbit ran off to the farmyard for an egg.

The Mouse unlocked her store cupboard and took out the remaining pieces of cheese rind, which she was keeping for another day.

She baked and she cooked, and she made her macaroni cheese. This one was six times as big as the first, for she made it in her washing-tub. It was juicy with cheese, and spiky with stalks of mouse-macaroni. Tim Rabbit helped her to carry it to the foot of the tree.

The delicious smell rose higher and higher, piercing the branches, floating up among the leaves till it reached the nose of the Owl.

'A smell of cooking! It reminds me of my mother, at home in the farmer's barn, when we had plenty of cheese and bacon.'

He sniffed dreamily, and shut his eyes again.

'Give me back my children,' cried the Mouse.

He roused himself and stared down. The great dish

lay below him, thin spirals of rich smells came from it. The Owl snapped his beak and blinked.

There sat Tim Rabbit, and a Hedgehog, a Frog, and a Snail, all staring up at him.

'Is that you, Tim Rabbit?' he hooted.

'Yes, Owl. Give her back her children. She's made a dinner for you,' piped little Tim Rabbit, waving his paws.

'Take thy children,' suddenly the Owl cried. He tossed the cradle in the air, and watched it float harmlessly down in the wind. After it panted the mother, the Hedgehog, Tim Rabbit, the Frog, and the little Snail with his house on his back. They all hurried to see the little round straw balloon. It came to rest among the flowers, and out of it tumbled six eager mice, waving their wooden spoons, talking of their adventure, proud of their aeroplane flight.

Down flew the Owl on silent wings, and he ate the tasty dish spread out for him. Nobody looked at him. They were all looking at the little mice. The Frog began to turn somersaults to make the little mice laugh. The Hedgehog rattled his prickles. The Snail popped into his house and then popped out again. Tim Rabbit picked up one of the macaroni stalks and tootled a song on it. Mrs Harvest Mouse spread the forget-me-not blue cot-cover on the ground.

When at last Tim Rabbit went home, the family of mice had gone to bed, tucked under the coverlet, each with a rattle in its fist.

'Cony cheese. Cony cheese,' they were murmuring

*Tim Rabbit helped her to carry it to the foot of
the tree*

as they shut their eyes and curled up into a ball in the straw nest.

'I want some cony cheese,' said Tim, when he got home to his mother.

'Cony cheese?' asked Mrs Rabbit. 'What's that?'

'A dinner that makes even the Owl forget,' answered Tim, and he told his mother all about it.

V. Tim Rabbit and the Slipper

Tim Rabbit was running down the short cut between the hedge and the lane when he spied something white shining in the grass.

'It's a funny-shaped mushroom,' said he, picking up the small object. 'A nice white mushroom with a button on its stalk.'

He turned it over. There were two little straps of white kid, and a tiny white button and a white silk pompom.

'Here's a thing and a very pretty thing,' sang Tim, dangling it in his paw. 'What shall I do with this pretty thing?'

He carried it home to his mother. Mrs Rabbit was doing the ironing. She turned from her table full of clean clothes to greet her son.

'Come along, Tim. Did you have a nice run?' she asked, smiling at her small son. 'What have you got behind your back?'

Tim held out the pretty thing.

'Oh, Mother! See what I found, down the lane on our own private pathway!' he cried. 'What is it? Have you ever seen such a cury-curyous thing?'

Mrs Rabbit put her iron back on the fire, and took the little slipper. She stroked the soft kid and rubbed the silky pompom on her cheek.

'It's a baby's slipper, Tim. A real live baby's slipper lost from a little foot, kicked away by someone very young.'

'A slipper-slopper? A real one, for a human baby?'

'Yes. Five little pink toes lived here,' said Mrs Rabbit, dreamily, as she gazed at the soft white slipper.

'Like baby mice in a nest?' asked Tim.

Mrs Rabbit didn't answer. She was trying to remember where she had seen a little baby lying on its back kicking its legs. On the tiny feet were white slippers with fluffy pompoms.

'One, two, buckle my shoe,' said Tim, fastening the button, and then throwing up the slipper and catching it.

'Now I remember, Tim,' exclaimed Mrs Rabbit. 'It belongs to Baby Bunting, the son of Eli Bunting the cobbler. He lives in the ivy-covered cottage at the end of the lane. Mrs Bunting will be upset about this slipper. Take it back, Tim, and put it on the doorstep.'

'Shall I fill it with buttercups and daisies?' asked Tim.

'Yes, and a wisp of lamb's wool from the hedges would be useful to keep the baby's toes warm,' said Mrs Rabbit. 'Take it back now, Tim. The baby will want his slipper.'

Tim ran outside with the little white slipper clutched in his paw. He trotted across the common to the fields, and then put it in the leaves of a large dock plant while he gathered buttercups and daisies and looked for lamb's wool. There it lay, half-hidden by the long leaves, but somebody saw it.

The stout old Toad who kept the inn at the hedge-bottom waddled slowly up and examined the little white slipper.

'Hm!' said he. 'Hm! Just the thing for my inn. I want a new sign to hang at the door. I'm tired of "Pig

and Whistle". I'll call my inn "The Baby's Slipper".
Yes, it will bring me new customers. It's just what I
want.'

He carried it off, and when Tim came back with
his flowers and lamb's wool the Toad was far away.
Tim went sadly home, but the fat old Toad staggered
happily along to his inn door. He hung the white
slipper with a horse hair to the tree at the doorway.
He took down the old sign of the 'Pig and Whistle'.

'The sign of "The Baby's Slipper",' said he, pointing it out to his friends.

Everyone who came to sip the good honeymead
which the Toad kept in his wooden barrel looked up
at the hanging slipper.

'You've got a fine homely picture there, Neighbour
Toad,' said the animals, and Toad nodded his
head.

'Yes. It's the sign of family life and laughter and
all the good things of childhood,' said the Toad. 'It's
the sign of "The Baby's Slipper".'

The Hedgehog who came for a drink of the Toad's
honey-toddy stood for a long time staring up at the
dangling slipper. Then he pushed his long sharp
prickle into it and carried it off. When the Toad came
to the door the inn sign had gone. In the distance was
the Hedgehog walking away with it.

'Oh dear! I shall have to use my old sign again,'
sighed the Toad, and he fished it out of the ditch and
hung it up.

'This will make a good basket for my wife's shopping,' said the Hedgehog. 'She wants a new basket. She's always asking for one. Always bothering me.'

Mrs Hedgehog was delighted. She hung the strap over her arm, and then she went to do the family shopping with the new basket. She filled the slipper with tender green leaves and young shoots, and a fat juicy snail and a few grubs.

Everybody stared at her. 'Look at Mrs Hedgehog with her new shopping-basket!' they cried. 'Isn't it fine? It isn't made from rushes or straw or grass. It's made of fine white leather, soft as silk. See how she carries it on her arm with no trouble at all!'

Mrs Hedgehog strutted along the market places, very proud of herself and her basket. When it was full she took it home. She emptied the food on the kitchen table and hung the basket on a twig at her front door. She wanted all who passed by to admire her new basket.

Unluckily for Mrs Hedgehog a wandering Hen saw it. With a cluck of surprise she seized it, and popped it on her head.

'A white bonnet, all trimmed with a silky pom-pom in the latest fashion,' said she. 'Bonnet strings too, and a button to fasten it. Never was there such good fortune!'

She ran as fast as her legs could carry her, back to the farmyard. How she ran! She ran so fast that the bonnet fell off but she didn't know. When she got to the farm she called the hens around her.

'Look at my new bonnet,' she boasted. Then she

She ran as fast as her legs could carry her

put up her claw, and discovered the bonnet was lost. That was very sad, for it really suited her. She looked charming in that bonnet.

The baby's slipper did not lie long in the field. A Magpie spied it, and darted down with a shriek of joy.

'A treasure! A snow-white treasure! I shall use it to fly on my nest. A white flag on my airy castle.'

The Magpie flew away to its nest, and hung the little white slipper on the high bough of the tree. There it swung in the wind and rain. To and fro it swayed, and the Magpie was proud to have a shining flag on its castle walls.

The wind blew hard that night, and the little white slipper sailed away. Down, down it fluttered, right down to the cornfield. It dropped like a feather close to the nest of Mrs Harvest Mouse.

'Oh, look what the wind has brought me,' she cried, putting her head out of her window. 'Look! A cradle for my babies.'

She ran round and round the slipper, tasting the pompom, licking the button, sniffing at the soft leather. Then she hung it on a cornstalk. In it she put her young family of tiny mice. They curled up in a pink ball, with close-shut eyes and slept soundly in that baby's slipper.

All day they slept, and the Mouse was able to clean her house and wash the floor and dust the straw walls. It was very grand to have a nursery near, and to be free from domestic worries. She even ventured away for a minute to visit her friend. When she came back the cradle had gone and the little mice were rolling over and over on the hard ground.

'Who has done this?' she asked indignantly.

'I did. It's just what I want for a nut-bowl,' said a Squirrel, and there was nothing the Mouse could do

but to put the babies back in the straw house.

Away went the Squirrel, to a fir-tree. She picked three little fir-cones, and the basket was filled completely. She emptied them out by her own tree, and went out again to pick nuts. She gathered many, and filled the tiny slipper. The baby's mother would hardly have recognized it now. It was a green-streaked little bag of nuts.

She dropped the slipper in the hole of the tree, and forgot about it. It might have been there now if somebody hadn't found it.

Tim Rabbit was poking about in the woods for anything he could find. He pushed his paw into the hole, for he saw the pile of shells outside where the Squirrel had feasted.

'Ah, Squirrel's larder!' said Tim, and he fumbled with his soft furry fist in the hollow. Out into the daylight he brought the soiled little slipper.

'A basket. A bag. A leather bag,' said Tim. He sniffed at it, and examined it.

'I do believe – I do believe – I do – I do. It *is*!'

Home he raced with the poor little slipper dangling on his arm by the strap, and the pompom like a wisp of rag.

'Mother! You'll never guess what I've found! You'll never, never guess!' he cried.

'What is it? A rag-bag?' asked Mrs Rabbit.

'Don't you know?' persisted Tim.

'Why, I do believe it's that baby's lost slipper!' cried Mrs Rabbit, turning over the slipper in her paws.

'Can we clean it and take it back?' asked Tim.

'Yes. I'll put it in my wash-tub and scrub it with my special soap,' said Mrs Rabbit.

She fetched a bunch of the pale pink flower called 'Soapwort', which you can find in the fields. It is the soap of long ages ago, but everyone has forgotten except the wood people.

She squeezed the strong juice from the stems on the slipper and scrubbed with a tiny brush of heather. The soapwort juice took away the dirt. She twisted the slipper in her paws and rubbed here and there till every green and brown stain had gone. Then she hung it by the fire, not too near and not too far, so that it dried slowly. Then she ironed it with her little flat-iron.

'It's not quite white,' said Tim, doubtfully. 'It's rather yellow, Mother. The pompom's fluffy now, but the slipper is a bit soiled and tired-looking.'

'Let the moon bleach it,' said Mrs Rabbit.

She hung it out in the moonlight that night, close to the door so that nobody would carry it away. The full moon looked down, and the moonbeams turned the slipper a dazzling white. It was just like a new slipper the next morning when Mrs Rabbit brought it indoors and set it on the table.

'Now you can take it back to Baby Bunting,' said she. 'And you might fill it with presents from your toy-cupboard.'

So Tim filled the tiny slipper with lots of jolly things. He put in it a basket carved from a cherry-stone, and a cup made from an acorn, a chair carved out of a chestnut, and a rattle made out of twisted green rushes with a pea inside. The little slipper was packed with the treasures. Lastly he wrote on a beech leaf the words, 'A present from No Ornery Rabit', and he fastened the leaf to the button on the strap.

Away he went, carefully carrying the slipper with its load of pretty things. Away he went to the cottage where the baby lived. There he lay, in his wicker cot, kicking his legs, and crooning to himself.

'Baby Bunting,' whispered Tim Rabbit.

The baby looked up at the sky, and down at the flowers, and he began to laugh and kick his bare legs faster than ever.

Tim stood on tiptoes and stretched up. He climbed to the cot, and held out the white slipper to the baby.

The cottage door opened and the mother came down the garden. Tim popped the slipper on the cot and dashed away.

'A rabbit! Could that possibly be a rabbit looking at baby?' asked Mrs Bunting, and she ran to the cot.

'Coo-oo-oo,' sang the baby.

'What's this? Your lost slipper, I declare! Full of little toys too,' said the astonished mother.

She looked about, but Tim had disappeared. She picked up the baby and the slipper and went back to the house.

'All these pretty things in our baby's slipper. They look like fairy toys,' said she to her husband.

'Where have they come from?' he asked, staring at the slipper.

'Brought by a rabbit, as clear as I could see,' she answered.

'A rabbit? It must have been little Tim Rabbit

then,' said he. 'I've heard tell of him. He's No Ordinary Rabbit.'

'Yes, here's the letter from him,' said Mrs Bunting, reading the leaf's message.

She placed the toys in the corner cupboard where they would be safe. Then she fetched the other slipper.

'The lost one looks as clean and nice as when it was bought,' said she, and she put the two little slippers on the baby's feet.

'Tim Rabbit! Tim! Tim! Coo-oo-oo!' chanted the baby, and he kicked his short legs and showed off his white slippers and the silky pompoms.

'There! He's talking. Those are his first words,' said his fond mother. 'Tim Rabbit!'

VI. Tim Rabbit's Handkerchief

It was Monday morning, and Mrs Rabbit was hanging out the washing and Tim was helping her. So nimble and quick was little Tim Rabbit, dodging under the small garments which fluttered on the bushes, so trim was Mrs Rabbit, with her sleeves rolled up! The East wind tossed the clothes, and the West wind fluttered them, and the North wind breathed on them and the South wind kissed them. In a few minutes they were dry, for they were like flowers hanging there.

'Fetch the clothes in for me, Tim,' called Mrs Rabbit from the doorway and Tim carried them in the small green rush basket. He dragged them off the broom bushes and the gorse, from the low hawthorns and the nut trees, and from the crooked little lavender bushes in the garden. He didn't notice one small green handkerchief, which lay on the last twisty little lavender bush. He didn't see it at all although it was his best Sunday handkerchief. So he carried the basketful of clothes indoors to his mother.

'Here's a jam pasty for you,' said Mrs Rabbit, patting his head. He took the three-cornered little pasty and skipped away with it, for the work was done and he was free to play.

Mrs Rabbit reached the smoothing-iron from the shelf and warmed it by the fire. She spread the clean clothes on the table and began to iron them. First of all she ironed the little rose-pink pyjamas belonging to Tim. Next she ironed her own forget-me-not blue nightgown. Then she ironed Tim's foxglove-coloured jacket, which he wore on Sundays.

Then she ironed her own green print frock, spotted with dark marks, like the leaves of the Wake Robin. Then she ironed Mr Rabbit's dead-leaf coat, and the trousers to match. She hunted in the bottom of the basket for Tim's green handkerchief. It wasn't there. She looked on the floor, under the table. She went out of doors and searched among the bushes.

'I hung it on the old lavender bush, I remember,' said she to herself. 'I did, I'm certain.'

Away in the distance she could see little Tim leaping over the stones, jumping from the fallen tree trunk, and swinging on the low bough of the nut tree.

'Of course. I expect Tim carried it off,' said she, and she went back to the house to finish ironing the towels and pillow-cases and little white sheets.

But Tim hadn't carried it off. Nobody knew where it had gone.

'There's no footprints here,' said Tim, lying down and peeping under the lavender bush. 'There's no mark of a slug or a snail or a weasel or a toad.'

'Somebody's taken it,' said Mrs Rabbit. 'Never

mind. I'll make you another out of a primrose leaf.'

She gathered a primrose leaf, which is soft as velvet to a bunny's nose. She nibbled it nicely into a square with an embroidered edge. It had a sweet scent of its own, and it needed no perfume upon it.

'Thank you, Mother,' said Tim, putting it in his pocket. Although it was very pretty, and soft and green, it wasn't as nice as his beloved Sunday hanky.

He kept his eyes wide open whenever he went down the lanes, or across the fields, or up the hills, or through the woods. He asked everybody he met about it.

'Have you seen a green hanky, soft as silk and green as grass?' he asked the prickly Hedgehog.

'Yes. There are hundreds of hankies in the hedge bottom,' said the Hedgehog.

So Tim ran there and looked about. It was true the lane was covered with green handkerchiefs, fastened to the cowslips and red campion and cuckoo flowers. It was littered with handkerchiefs belonging to the nut trees and rose bushes and foxgloves. It was carpeted with thousands of handkerchiefs, but there was never a one as nice as Tim's own lost handkerchief.

'Why can't you take one of these?' asked Tim's cousin Jane. 'They are lovely and they smell 'licious.'

'They aren't like mine,' said Tim, shortly. 'These wither and wrinkle after a week's wear, but mine lasts for ever.'

'Well, it's gone now,' said Jane.

'You needn't remind me,' said Tim. Jane was

rather stupid at times, he thought, considering she was his cousin.

One day Tim and Jane went farther away from their homes than they had ever been. They went up a field, and across a pasture and over a brook, using little stepping-stones and hopping over the water. The grass in the pasture above the brook was sweet and good. They ate quite a large dinner. Then they played hide-and-seek among the black stones, where ferns and brambles made splendid hiding-places.

Jane hid her fat little self in a clump of foxglove leaves and Tim couldn't find her. He ran in and out and round about the stones. Then he saw something that made him hold his breath with excitement. Fastened to two foxglove stems was a thin clothes-line of horsehair, and on it hung Tim's own green handkerchief. It swung there with some of the smallest clothes Tim had ever seen. They were scarlet and blue and green, as delicate as cobweb, and they could have been packed in a thimble.

Tim stretched out a paw and grabbed his hanky. The whole line of clothes fell down and wrapped itself about his shoulders. At the same time a peal of bells rang, every foxglove tinkled an alarm, and as the foxgloves were tall and covered with dark red bells, there was a noise like a cathedral o' Sundays, only of course it was a small noise, which only a rabbit could hear.

'Who's taking my washing? Who's stealing my clothes?' cried a wee small voice, shrill and high.

Tim looked around but he couldn't see anyone.

Jane Rabbit came out of her hiding-place, looking rather frightened.

'What's the matter, Tim?' she asked. 'Why are all those bells jingling?' she asked, pointing to the shaking foxgloves that shook as if the wind were inside them. The pollen flew and made her sneeze.

'Thief! Thief!' squeaked the small voice.

'Thief yourself,' said Tim stoutly. 'It's my hanky.'

'Who is it?' whispered Jane Rabbit, clutching Tim's jacket.

'It's – it's – I can't see anybody,' stammered Tim. The green line was twisted round his neck and the tiny garments tickled his chin and nose.

'Is it a Bumble-bee? Is it a Hornet?' asked Jane, peering into the dark bushes.

'Hornet! Bumble-bee!' shrieked the wee small voice, and a small pointed dart, sharp as a needle, whizzed past Jane's head and struck her arm.

'Put my sheet down,' shouted the invisible one.

'Sheet? It's my hanky,' shouted Tim indignantly. 'Come out and let me see you.'

'Here I am, right under your broad nose and your stupid eyes,' said the voice.

Tim looked closer at the foxglove in front of him. There, peeping from behind a leaf, was a small fellow, no bigger than Tim's foot.

'It's a dwarf,' whispered Jane, and away she galloped helter-skelter, all the way home, leaving Tim to face the elfin person all by himself.

'What have you to say, carrying off my washing?' asked the dwarf.

'Please, sir, it's my little green hanky, that I lost. Somebody took it from the lavender bush.'

'Indeed. That's where I found it,' remarked the small figure and he stroked his beard and stared at Tim with eyes like fire.

'You can have it back again, Tim Rabbit, on one condition.'

'Yes, sir?' said Tim, who was surprised at the little creature knowing his name.

'At the bottom of this field, on a mound of good grass, you'll find a fairy ring. You know what that is?'

'Yes, sir. A ring of little toadstools, with plenty of room in the middle for sports and dancing, but we rabbits don't go inside.'

'There's a horseshoe lying near, too close for our comfort. I want you to take it away. As long as it lies there we can't have our games.'

'Yes, sir, but why, sir?' asked Tim.

'Iron, my young ignorant friend, is a powerful force. We dwarfs and fairies can't go near it. It keeps us off. So get rid of it, and you can have your green handkerchief back.'

'I'll go and look at it and take it away,' said Tim, hopefully.

He scampered down the pasture, and soon he found the fairy ring. It was a beautiful circle of toadstools, with soft short grass and purple wild thyme, and blue milkwort growing there. Close to the ring was a great horseshoe.

'What have you to say, carrying off my washing?'
asked the dwarf

It was so heavy Tim couldn't even lift one corner. He tried and he tried, but it wouldn't budge. Nothing would make it move. As he was pushing and dragging at it, the Hedgehog came up.

'What are you doing, Tim Rabbit?' he asked.

'Trying to move this horseshoe from the fairy ring,' answered Tim, wiping the sweat from his face.

'And why do you want to move it?' asked the Hedgehog.

'So that the fairy man can dance again. He's got my green hanky, and he won't give it back till I move this shoe,' said Tim.

So the Hedgehog pushed and pulled, but together they could not move it.

Up came a small field Mouse.

'What are you doing, Hedgehog and Tim Rabbit?' she asked.

'Trying to move this horseshoe from the fairy ring,' they said.

'Why are you doing that?' she asked.

'So that the fairy man can dance again,' answered Tim.

So the little Mouse helped Hedgehog and Tim. The Mouse shoved, and Tim pulled and the Hedgehog heaved, but never a bit did that horseshoe move.

Then little Jane came hopping through the pasture looking for Tim.

'What are you and Hedgehog and Mouse doing?' she asked.

'Trying to move this horseshoe from the fairy ring,' answered Tim.

'Why do you want to do that?' she asked.

'So that the fairy man can dance again,' said Tim.

They tugged and pulled, all except Jane, who sat on the horseshoe, dangling her legs. Of course the shoe didn't move, and they all sat down and mopped their faces, and shook their heads.

Then the Mole came heaving out of the ground, and he stared at the company.

'What are you doing, Hedgehog, and Tim, Mouse and Jane?' he asked.

'Trying to move this horseshoe from the fairy ring,' they answered.

'Why do you want to move it?' asked the Mole.

'So that the fairy man can dance here again,' said Tim.

'I don't touch steel or iron,' said the Mole. 'I can't help you. Mole traps are made of iron, and we Moles keep away from the cold metal. But I have something stronger than iron.'

He disappeared in the grass, and wriggled his body down into the soil. They sat waiting, and the birds sang, and the clouds scudded across the sky. The Mole returned with a piece of stone, smooth as if it had been in a very hot fire.

'This is a loadstone,' said he. 'It came out of the sky. It fell down one day, and was half buried and I dug it up.'

'What's it for?' asked Tim.

'You'll see,' answered the Mole. He pushed the loadstone towards the horseshoe, and a strange thing happened. The shoe began to move. Over the grass

*Then little Jane came hopping through the pasture
looking for Tim*

moved the shoe, away it went, till it touched the loadstone. There it clung and nobody could get the two
apart.

'It's a magnet,' explained the Mole. 'It draws iron
and makes it follow.'

'Now I can fetch the fairy man,' cried Tim joyfully.

'Wait till we've gone home,' said the Mole. 'He
might take a piece of my fur coat for a blanket.'

'He might take one of my prickles for a spear,' said
the Hedgehog.

'He might snip off my tail and use it for a whip,' said the Mouse.

'I'll stay with you. I'm not afraid now,' said Jane.

So Tim and Jane galloped up the pasture to the little Dwarf. There he was, swinging on the line among his washing, turning somersaults, and tight-rope walking on the thin black horsehair.

'Are you defeated?' he asked Tim.

'I'm never quite defeated,' said Tim. 'Please give me my hanky, and you can go and dance in your fairy ring.'

'Take it and be off with you. Don't go leaving it about,' said the fairy man.

He flew away to the ring and in a minute he was wildly dancing there, calling to his friends in briar and bramble.

Tim Rabbit put the green handkerchief in his pocket, and took Jane's paw. They scampered across the stepping-stones, down the fields, home to the common.

'I've got my old green hanky, Mother. The fairy man had taken it,' announced Tim, flinging open the cottage door.

'A fairy man? Oh, Tim, you might have been be-witched into a cow, or a stump, or a butterfly,' said Mrs Rabbit. 'It was very risky.'

'Can we have muffins for tea, in honour of it?' asked Tim.

Mrs Rabbit smiled and nodded to the two. She was glad Tim had found his own handkerchief again. But it was never quite the same. It had strange habits, such as hiding under cushions, or flying up in the air, or fluttering about like a bird and settling on a bush. Tim had to hold it tightly, and stuff it deep in his pocket, or it might have flown right away, back to the fairy man.

VII. Tim Rabbit goes Camping

One morning when Tim Rabbit went for his usual ramble across the common, he saw something new. He started in surprise and then tiptoed towards the strange white thing. It wasn't a stray cow, or a snowy haystack, or a house, or even a sheet blown away from somebody's orchard washing-line. It didn't walk, but it billowed and shook in the wind. Tim crept softly up, stopping now and then to sniff the splendid smells that drifted over the common.

'What is it?' he whispered to the Hedgehog, who sauntered out of the hedge. 'What's that big white flower as big as a thorn bush?'

'It's a tent,' said the Hedgehog, who knew everything. 'It's a house with somebody living inside.'

'It wasn't there last night,' Tim whispered loudly. 'I 'member running over that way and nibbling the daisies. Houses can't fly, can they?'

'No, Tim, but this came on a bicycle. There's the machine covered up near. You had better keep away or the camper might put you in his cooking-pot and boil you in a savoury stew.'

The Hedgehog shook his head at Tim to warn him.

'You're a foolish young rabbit, Tim, so be careful,' he added.

So Tim went very carefully, making a large circle round the tent till he came to the doorway. The camper was there, sitting on a little stool, frying bacon in a frying-pan over his Primus stove.

Tim Rabbit was so excited he forgot to hide and he sat up to sniff. Delicious smells arose and faint smoke twirled in the bushes. Tim sniffed and sniffed with his little soft nose. It was as good as having breakfast. He watched every movement of the camper. He saw a couple of eggs cracked and dropped into the frying-pan, and boiling water poured into a coffee-pot, and even crunchy toast made.

When breakfast was finished the camper lighted a cigarette and came outside to the stream. Tim Rabbit thought it was time to be going home. So off he scampered, with his little white tail bobbing and his ears laid flat.

He told his mother all about it.

'Eggs and bacon and coffee, Mother.'

'Now be sensible, Tim. Don't make free with campers,' warned Mrs Rabbit.

The next morning Tim Rabbit invited some of his friends to view the camper. They were just in time to see the man pack up the white tent on a bicycle and ride away. It was a disappointment to Tim, but when he ran to the patch of grass where the tent had stood the air was full of smells. Clouds of bacon and egg smells hovered in the dell; smells of hot coffee came whiffing from the rocks, where the coffee grains had been thrown away; smells of tomato sauce and beans came from the bushes, and a delicate aroma of burnt porridge drifted from an old pan thrown away in the heather. Tim enjoyed everything.

'Come along everybody and share the fun,' he called, and the timid ones who had remained hidden while the bold little rabbit looked about, now came up.

Sniff! Sniff! Sniff! they went, poking their noses here and there.

'Here's another fine smell. Here's another,' they cried, as they leapt among the heather. The camper had left so many nice cooking smells behind him that the rabbits got quite fat upon them.

They ran about looking for empty tins, licking the sticky milk and the sweet syrup and the sour vinegar, and thick oil. They poked their noses into every nook and corner, finding a lump of sugar that had been dropped, a crust of bread, and an empty bottle that had a very strong odour. Tim Rabbit felt rather dizzy when he tilted up the last drop of liquid. He even had to lie down and be covered with a blanket of leaves till he recovered his wits.

'It's something the camper had to polish his boots,' said he.

Then he found a tin spoon, and he beat on a tin, like a drum. His cousin Jane made a mouth-organ out of a couple of squeaker grasses, and they all had some music.

'I shall go camping,' said Tim Rabbit.

'And me! And me!' cried every animal on the common.

Tim Rabbit ran home at last, for the sun was high in the sky, and every crumb and morsel of food had been eaten by rabbits and birds and ants.

'I've had my breakfast, Mother,' said he. 'I licked tins left by the camper.'

'That's for scavengers, like crows and beetles, not for good little rabbits,' scolded Mrs Rabbit.

'I want to go camping, Mother,' said he.

'You can't go camping, my son,' said Mrs Rabbit. 'You're too little. You'd be lonely.'

'I'd take Cousin Jane and Sam Hare,' said Tim.

'What would you eat?' asked Mrs Rabbit.

'Bits and bobs,' replied Tim.

'Where would you get the tent from?' asked Mrs Rabbit.

'Somewhere. There must be one somewhere,' said Tim, looking rather puzzled. He hadn't thought of that.

'Rabbits don't go camping,' said Mrs Rabbit, sternly.

'This rabbit does,' whispered Tim, and off he went, to look for a tent.

He met the Hedgehog moving gloomily through the leaves under the hedge, kicking up his toes and grumbling.

'Somebody's gone and eaten all those bits of white

bread,' said the Hedgehog crossly to Tim. 'Somebody's been to the camper's place.'

'Oh! Oh! Where can I find a tent, Hedgehog?' asked Tim.

'What do you want a tent for? Tents aren't for you,' said the Hedgehog gruffly.

'To go camping, of course,' said Tim.

'Rabbits don't go camping. Rabbits don't do it, and they don't eat the bits and bobs either,' said the Hedgehog.

'This rabbit does,' said Tim.

The Hedgehog frowned, and shook his fist, but it was only in fun and Tim ran off laughing.

He asked many of his friends about a tent, and nobody took any notice of his foolish questions.

'I'll go and ask Aunt Eliza,' thought Tim. 'She's wiser, is Aunt Lizer, than me.'

He sang as he went:

> 'Aunt Eliza is wiser, is wiser than me.
> She's wiser, she's wiser than me.'

When he got to Aunt Eliza's house he tapped at the door, and pulled up the bobbin and lifted the latch and walked in.

Aunt Eliza sat by the fire with her head wrapped up in brown paper.

'Good morning, Aunt Eliza,' cried Tim cheerfully. 'Here's your nephew Tim to see you.'

'I've got the ear-ache, Tim,' moaned Aunt Eliza. 'Oh dear-a-me! I've put hot brown paper round my ears, but it doesn't cure me.'

'I know a cure for ear-ache,' said Tim. 'It's rabbit leaves. I'll go and get some for you. You put them on. My mother cured my ear-ache that way.'

'Oh, Tim!' cried Aunt Eliza, rocking to and fro with pain. 'Oh, Tim, my favourite nephew Tim, go and fetch some rabbit leaves.'

So Tim ran through the green pathways to the rough tangle where grew the tall mullein flowers with their soft furry leaves. He picked a bunch of the long leaves, and stroked them gently. They were like velvet. Then he bit off a spike of the yellow flowers, and bore it like a golden flag.

'It will do for my tent pole when I find the tent,' said he.

He hurried back with the rabbit leaves tucked under his arms and the tall spike of flowers held aloft.

'Stop and play,' called a friend. 'Tim, Tim.'

Everybody was beckoning him, but he wouldn't stop. He pulled the bobbin and ran into the cottage.

'Here you are, Aunt Eliza,' said he, offering the rabbit leaves.

Aunt Eliza removed the brown paper from her head and wrapped the long soft leaves round her ears. Tim tied them with a handkerchief, and fastened the knot well.

'That's better. I feel less achy already,' said Aunt Eliza with a smile.

'There's nothing like rabbit leaves for ear-ache,' said Tim.

'And wild sage for tooth-ache and rose leaves for head-ache,' added Aunt Eliza.

'There's nothing like rabbit leaves for ear-ache,'
said Tim

Tim was wandering round the room, looking at the picture of Uncle Benjamin, Aunt Eliza's late husband, turning the egg-boiler upside down, touching the swinging bunches of herbs and the string of onions and dried rose leaves and wild thyme. They dangled from the ceiling and tickled his ears as he went under them. Tim was thinking deeply, wondering about the tent. Then he spoke.

'Aunt Eliza,' said he at last. 'I want a tent. Where can I find one?'

'A tent?' Aunt Eliza sat back in her rocking-chair, and rocked and rocked while she considered the matter. The green bandage round her ears made such a queer shadow Tim couldn't help laughing.

'What's the matter, Tim?' asked Aunt Eliza, rather crossly.

'Your shadow, Aunt Eliza. It's like a donkey. Such long ears you have.'

'Yours isn't much better, Tim,' said his Aunt and she pointed to another odd-looking fellow on the rough old wall.

'Let me see,' she added. 'What's a tent for? I quite forget. I'm getting old, and I forget these modern inventions.'

'It's to camp in. To fry your breakfast in the doorway and to look out at the world,' said Tim eagerly.

'Oh yes! I've seen one in the field, down by Farmer Green's. You could have a tent made of thistledown, Tim. I'll make you one on my spinning-wheel. I'm a good spinner. I made the blankets for your mother when she was married, from sheep's wool in the hedges. I'll make you a tent all for yourself, Tim.'

'Oh, Aunt Eliza,' murmured Tim and he hugged his old Aunt till she squeaked for breath, and the green rabbit leaves fell off.

'Go and get some thistledown and I'll set to work,' she said. 'My ear-ache has gone, and I'm feeling grand.'

Away ran Tim to his friends in field and lane.

'Thistledown to make a tent,' he shouted as he rushed among them. 'A tent! Hurrah! You shall all come and stay with me.'

'Can I? Can I? Can I?' they called, pressing round their leader.

'All who get thistledown shall come,' promised Tim.

So every little rabbit and hedgehog and squirrel, and young Sam Hare too, nipped about among the tall thistles that grew in the deserted field. Soon they had pulled the soft white down from every purple thistle head. The farmer was very glad when he saw that the thistle-seed had gone, but he didn't know who had taken it. They filled their baskets, they filled their sacks, and little Tim Rabbit carried the great ball of snowy thistledown back to his Aunt's cottage.

The ball was so big that the down filled the kitchen, and overflowed into the bedroom through the open doorway.

'Click! Clack!' went the spinning-wheel, and Aunt Eliza tapped with her foot. 'Click! Clack!' went the loom, and Aunt Eliza threw the shuttle backwards and forwards.

At last it was finished, and Aunt Eliza held out a piece of silky stuff.

'Hang this on your tent pole, and it'll make a lovely

tent, light as a feather, warm as a bird's nest,' said she.

So Tim put up the silver-white tent on the common, near his home, and there he went each morning to cook his breakfast and invite his friends. He would have lived there all summer if a grey Donkey had not wandered that way. The Donkey gave a little snort of glee, and ate up the whole tent.

'Thistledown is my favourite breakfast,' said he to Tim. 'What's yours?'

'Carrots,' said Tim, crossly. 'You've been and eaten me out of house and home, Neddy.'

'Go back to your mother, Tim Rabbit,' advised the Donkey. 'If I hadn't eaten your tent, then the Fox might have seen it and made a breakfast of you. He's had his eye on you and your thistledown tent.'

Tim glanced hurriedly round. There was the Fox peeping from the bushes, watching the Donkey and Tim. Tim didn't wait any longer. He thought it was time to go home to his mother.

VIII. Tim Rabbit and the Magical Bonnet

One fine misty morning Tim Rabbit went out early to gather mushrooms. Mrs Rabbit made very tasty mushroom stews, and Tim knew a good mushroom field. He started off in high spirits, with his basket on his arm. He ran with a hop and a skip through the dewy grass, leaving tiny footprints in the gossamer webs. Everything had a magical air on that bright day, when the moon had only just faded and the stars were waiting somewhere up in the sky.

There were many mushrooms, white as snow, gleaming frostily in the wet grass. They had pale pink gills, and tiny frills round their stalks. Tim Rabbit ran here and there picking them and popping them into his rush-basket. Soon the basket was full, and Tim swung it on his arm to go home. He was walking back to the gate, stepping among the mushrooms that he had to leave behind, when he saw a tremendous mushroom, nearly as big as the famous mushroom umbrella under which he once walked in the rain.

'I *must* have this one,' said Tim to himself. 'I'll take this one even if I have to tie a string to it and drag it along.'

He stooped to the ground and drew the knobby root from the earth. In triumph he held up the lovely mushroom. It had a skin like white satin, and there was a pearly glow over it, as if it were alight. He twirled it round his head and rainbows seemed to float in the air about it. Then he heard a voice, high and strange like music and harp strings.

'Tim Rabbit! Tim Rabbit!' it called.

Tim looked high and he looked low, but he saw nobody. He glanced to the right and to the left, but all he could see was the old mare feeding in the distance.

'Tim Rabbit!' piped the wee voice.

Tim twisted round and cranked his neck to look on every side at once. Nobody can see a fairy if the fairy doesn't want to be seen.

'Who is it?' asked Tim, for he was dizzy with peeping and prying.

'Give me back my mushroom,' said the fairy. It was one of those little folk who hide in the fields unseen by human people, and seldom seen even by animals.

'That I won't,' said Tim. 'I can't see you, but whoever you are, ladybird or butterfly, or gnat or ant, hiding from me, and thinking you are so clever, I won't give you my mushroom. Finding's keeping.'

He picked up the basket with one paw and held the big mushroom with another, but, oh dear! sparks flew and lights glittered, and his hair seemed to stand on end, as if it were electric.

'Something queer about that place,' shivered Tim, and he hurried away. He didn't see the little fairy come flying with outspread wings transparent as air, to settle on the mushroom. He knew nothing about it at all, for even when he scrambled under the gate he didn't see the fairy sitting on the great mushroom top.

But the fairy was there all right. It had a frown on its small pointed face, and its wild eyes flashed with anger at Tim Rabbit. It stamped its small foot and shook its tiny fist at Tim. Every time it stamped Tim looked surprised.

'This mushroom seems heavy. It shakes,' thought Tim. 'There's a buzzing going on. I must have brought a bee.'

He went into the little house on the common to his mother and put the big mushroom on the floor.

'There, Mother! Look what I've brought. Now we can have a stew. And look at the big mushroom, Mother. It's big enough for a table.'

Mrs Rabbit left her cooking and came to Tim.

'What a lot you've found, Tim! And what a beauty that one is! It shines like silver.'

She picked up the fairy mushroom and the little fairy shook its wings and flew round the room buzzing with rage.

'What's that noise?' asked Mrs Rabbit. 'Has a Bumble-bee come in?'

'Give me back my mushroom,' squeaked the tiny elf.

'It's a something that wants its mushroom back,'

said Tim hurriedly. 'It's my own mushroom, and I won't give it back.'

Mrs Rabbit looked rather alarmed, for she could see nothing. The fairy flew to the door and stood poised on tiptoe, with the sunlight falling on its wings. Then Mrs Rabbit and Tim saw it.

'It's a fairy,' cried Mrs Rabbit, and Tim whisked his handkerchief to catch it. Away flew the lovely creature, up towards the sun, and Tim and his mother stared after it.

'Well, it's gone, so I'll get on with my work,' said Mrs Rabbit. 'I've never been so near a fairy before. It's perhaps a good thing we didn't catch it, for they're queer-tempered creatures, and apt to behave in strange ways. When I was young I heard that my grandmother once helped a fairy, and ever after the fairies have been kind, although this one had a bad temper.'

'It's because I took its table,' said Tim.

'Now come along, Tim, and forget all about that fairy. Go and fetch some herbs for the mushroom stew. I must put it on or dinner will be late.'

She emptied the basket and began to peel the little white mushrooms, and put them in the pot. The big fairy mushroom lay in the corner, shining with its own soft radiance.

Tim ran to the herb garden on the common. There, in a sunny spot among delicate harebells, grew many sweet-scented plants. He picked the purple flowers of wild thyme, and sprays of marjoram, and strong-smelling grey sage leaves. There was wild parsley too on the banks, and sorrel leaves with their sour cool taste.

So Mrs Rabbit made the stew and very nice it was. Tim lay all afternoon, basking in the sunshine, dreaming of the fairy and the good mushroom stew.

'We will have the big mushroom tomorrow,' said Mrs Rabbit. 'I'll make a mushroom pudding out of it, for a treat.'

When the table was cleared and the dinner things washed up, Mrs Rabbit brought the big fairy mushroom out of the corner, and sat down to peel it. She dragged at the satiny skin, and away it came all in one piece.

'Just look at this!' she called to Tim. 'This mushroom skin is beautiful! Come here, Tim.'

Tim came running to see. There was a scent of many sweet flowers in the room, and the mushroom skin lay on the table, like silver cloth.

'It would make something, Mother,' cried Tim, excitedly. 'It would make a pair of slippers, only I don't want any. It would make a pair of gloves, but we don't wear them. I know! It would make a bonnet for you, Mother. Would you like that?'

'A bonnet!' said Mrs Rabbit. 'Oh, Tim! It's years since I had a new bonnet. I *would* like one. Just a pretty little bonnet, with a rose at the side, and a green grass ribbon round it. Oh, Tim!'

Her eyes sparkled, and she clapped her paws with delight. She spread the mushroom skin on the table and measured it with her little tape-measure. Then she took the bright scissors off the shelf where they had lain, wrapped up, ever since Tim Rabbit cut off all his fur with them.

'Can you do it, Mother? Can you make a bonnet?' asked Tim.

'Yes, Tim,' said Mrs Rabbit proudly, and she cut the mushroom skin and twisted it into a bonnet of delicate shape.

Tim Rabbit went out to the common to find a wild rose and some broad grasses for ribbons. He made a little nosegay to put at the side of the bonnet – a few pansies and a daisy and rose.

Mrs Rabbit pinned them to the bonnet with a thorn, and she sewed the bonnet strings with fine grass thread. Then she put the bonnet on her head and stepped outside to view herself in the pond, for that was her looking-glass.

'Oh, Mother! You do look fine,' cried Tim, running after her. 'Oh, Mother, you do – you do – Oh, Mother, where are you?'

Mrs Rabbit had completely disappeared!

'I'm here, Tim. Why are you calling me?' said a voice close to him.

'Mother! Mother! I can't see you,' cried Tim, staring round. A paw touched his arm and made him jump.

'I'm here, Tim. What's the matter with you? Are you blind? I'm by your side, in my new bonnet, Tim.'

'Oh, Mother. I can't see you,' whimpered Tim.

Mrs Rabbit pinned them to the bonnet with a thorn

'That's strange. I can see myself. I've just been looking in the pond, and I look grand.'

She took off her bonnet and Tim flew to her arms.

'Oh, Mother! You went right away,' he cried.

'Nonsense, Tim! I was here all the time. I think your eyes must be wrong. I'll pick some eyebright flowers and make some lotion.'

She stooped to pick the little white speckled flowers of eyebright that clustered close to the ground, and she put her bonnet in safety on a bush. Tim picked it up and looked closely at it. It shone like silver, and when he twirled it round rainbow colours played over it. The rose was fairer than any flower he had ever seen, and the green ribbons were like bright glass.

He popped the bonnet on his head for a joke.

'Mother!' said he. 'Look at your Tim!' He chuckled and danced, and pretended to hold up his skirts.

'Tim!' cried Mrs Rabbit. 'Where are you hiding, Tim? Where are you, Tim?'

'I'm here, Mother,' laughed Tim.

'I can't see you, Tim,' said Mrs Rabbit, half-frightened.

'Then you must have some eyebright lotion, Mother,' said Tim. 'I'm here, under your nose. What's the matter today?'

He kissed his mother with a little soft kiss and tweaked her tail.

'Oh, Tim, I can't see you. And my bonnet has gone,' she said gravely.

Tim removed the bonnet and at once Mrs Rabbit saw him.

'Here it is, Mother,' said Tim, slowly. 'I believe it's a magical bonnet. Those who wear it can't be seen. Put it on again, Mother, and I'll tell you.'

Mrs Rabbit took the bonnet with shaking paws and put it on her little round head. She faded away like a shadow and nobody was there.

'You've gone,' cried Tim excitedly. 'Now take it off.'

She removed the bonnet, and there she was, her own stout comfortable self, with her apron round her waist and her shawl on her shoulders.

'It's an invisible bonnet,' cried Tim, leaping for joy. 'Now I can be an invisible rabbit like the Prince in the fairy-tale.'

'I don't want an invisible bonnet,' said Mrs Rabbit sadly gazing at her new bonnet. 'It's most disappointing. Here I was going to show myself to the neighbours, and they won't see me.'

'Think of the fun we can have!' cried Tim, slipping the bonnet on his head, and fading away.

'I don't want an invisible Tim,' said Mrs Rabbit. 'I don't like these magical tricks at all. No, indeed I don't.'

She stumped off home, and had a good cry. Then she made herself a cup of tea and felt better. Even when she found the rest of the mushroom had gone from the corner she didn't care.

'No more magics for me,' said she.

Tim ran off with the invisible bonnet on his head. He ran to Old Jonathan's school and snatched the reading book from somebody's paw. He stole an egg from a sitting hen. He crept up to his old enemy the Magpie and held its tail feathers, so that it squawked with fear. There seemed to be no end to the naughty tricks Tim Rabbit could play with his invisible bonnet on his head. Then Tim went too far. He got so bold he decided to visit the Fox in his den. That was very venturesome even for a rabbit with a fairy bonnet.

Tim walked up to the Fox's den, and pushed open the door. Now although he couldn't be seen, he was discovered by the wily Fox. Reynard the Fox was sitting in his chair, half asleep after a late night hunting. Suddenly a cold draught came and he saw the door move. He rose to his feet and licked his lips and padded to the door. He shut it, and sat down again.

Tim Rabbit tiptoed silently up to the Fox and actually pulled the thick red brush. That was indeed a rash thing to do! It is the first and last time a rabbit has ever pulled a fox's tail.

The Fox sprang up and lashed the air. Tim Rabbit danced away, but he could not resist taunting the Fox.

'Ha! Who is it?' he cried.

'That's the voice of Tim Rabbit,' barked the Fox. 'I'll catch you.'

The Fox made a grab at Tim, and Tim was frightened at that quick paw and those sharp teeth

*It is the first and last time a rabbit has ever pulled
a fox's tail*

and the red tongue so close to him. Poor Tim was chased over a chair, under the table, and round the room. At last, when he was weary and very tired, he managed to unlatch the door and escape. After him came the Fox, but Tim was safe. Away he ran on his four legs, his white tail bobbing. He didn't stop running till he got to the mushroom field.

'Oh dear! I never ran so fast before. He nearly got me!' he sighed, sinking to the grass.

He took off the bonnet and laid it on the ground near him, and fanned his hot face.

The wind came and blew the bonnet, gently moving it away. Tim stretched out his hand, but it fluttered from his grasp. He ran after it, but the bonnet went faster.

There was a flash of sunlight, and for a moment Tim saw the fairy dragging the bonnet by the green ribbons. Then up in the air it rose, and away over the treetops, and that was the last of it.

'A good thing too. We want no more fairy mushrooms in our house, Tim,' said Mrs Rabbit.

'Still, I did pull the Fox's tail,' laughed Tim.

IX. Tim Rabbit and the Fox

'Tim Rabbit. Run in the woods and gather some sticks for my fire,' said Mrs Rabbit as she sat at breakfast with Tim one morning. 'It's a fine day for stick-picking. There'll be lots of firewood lying about.'

'I'm not very good at picking up sticks,' faltered Tim, who really wanted to play with Sam Hare.

'Yes you are. You're the best picker-up of sticks I've ever known,' said Mrs Rabbit. 'You are so quick and so nimble, you can get a big bundle while other folk are just looking about them, waiting to begin.'

This pleased little Tim Rabbit.

'Will you bake me an apple-dumpling when I come home?' he asked.

'Yes, I will. A great enormous apple in a round soft dumpling, if you get a nice pile of sticks for my fire,' promised Mrs Rabbit.

Tim finished his breakfast and brought out a piece of rope to tie the wood and a sledge to pull it along.

'Mind the Fox, Tim,' warned Mrs Rabbit. 'Keep in our part of the wood, and don't go among those rocks and glades where he lives. Keep your eyes open for the Fox.'

'I don't care a button for the Fox,' laughed Tim, and away he scampered. He soon got to the wood and he found broken branches all over the place, for there had been a high wind in the night.

He tied the firewood in a bundle and put it on the sledge. Instead of going home he walked further into the wood. The sun shone through the trees upon an open glade, with silver birches and great beeches. The ground was green with thick soft moss, and a multitude of bluebells grew there. Tim went towards this lovely place, keeping an eye open for a fairy or a brown elf. There was a glint of water which reflected the sun like a looking-glass, and spickles and sparkles of light danced over the tree trunks.

'I might take one of those sparkles home with me,' thought Tim, and he stretched out his paw to catch the flickering sunshine.

He shaded his eyes, blinking away the dazzle of light, and he stepped lightly over the moss towards this enchanting place. Perhaps he thought he would see the fairies tripping there. If so, he was mistaken. Certainly somebody was dancing, but it was not a fairy. A tawny fellow, golden brown, was leaping there. The Fox it was, dancing for his little ones. They were rolling over and over with delight, and the Fox was playing a game with them.

Tim Rabbit was in a fright. He hoped they hadn't spied him. He started off, dodging among the shadowy bushes, stepping like a shadow himself. He peeped behind, and the Foxes were all dancing down the green moss. Tim thought they hadn't seen him, for

'He thinks I shan't catch him, but I shall'

they were tripping and turning like dancers at a fair with Mr Fox leading them. Tim slipped under his load of firewood, and hid under the dark shelter of the little sledge. They would never find him. He felt quite safe, but it was better to wait until they had passed by.

The Fox came leaping and prancing through the trees with his family dancing after him.

'Let us sit down on this pile of wood,' said the Fox to his cubs. 'You will be tired with romping so much.'

'We're not tired! Oh no!' cried the little Foxes. Tim shivered and shook as they all sat down upon the firewood. He kept very still, down there in the darkness.

'Are you quite comfy?' asked the Fox.

'Yes, Father. Oh, Father, tell us a story,' begged the cubs.

'What shall I tell you?' asked the Fox.

'Tell us about little Tim Rabbit,' they cried.

'Little Tim Rabbit is a bold young rabbit, and he lives with his mother and father in a house near the common,' said Mr Fox very loudly. 'He thinks I shan't catch him, but I shall.'

'Yes, you will,' laughed the little Foxes.

'He is No Ordinary Rabbit,' the Fox went on.

'No Ordinary Rabbit,' echoed the cubs.

'But I shall catch him some day,' said the Fox.

'Yes, Father. Oh, Father, has Tim Rabbit got wings?' asked one little Fox.

'Not yet,' said the Fox, grinning and showing his teeth.

'Then he can't fly?' asked another.

'No. He can fly a kite, but not fly himself,' explained the Fox.

Tim Rabbit couldn't help feeling proud at this. He chuckled to himself, and then he stuffed his paw in his mouth to keep back the laughter.

'He kept bees once. He has had his share of honey.'

'Will he taste very nice, Father? As nice as Duck?'

'Delicious! He is stuffed with sugar-plums is Tim Rabbit,' said Mr Fox.

Tim didn't feel so happy, as he listened. The little Foxes snapped their jaws and leapt with joy.

'Can we see Tim Rabbit, Father?' they asked.

'Yes, if you are good.'

'How will you catch him?' they asked.

'I shall put salt on his tail,' said the Fox.

'How will you cook him, Father?'

'Roast with apple-sauce and onion-pudding,' said the Fox. 'You go off and get some apples, my son. You go and find onions, my daughter. You fetch turnips, my youngest child, and you get potatoes, my second son.'

Away scampered the little ones, and the Fox gave a loud cough.

'You can come out now, Tim Rabbit,' said he. 'I want this firewood to cook you with.'

Out crept little Tim Rabbit feeling very scared. He remembered he was No Ordinary Rabbit and he tried to be brave. He looked at the Fox, and gave a little smile – rather a frightened little smile, it is true.

Then he looked up at the sky, and the sun was shining down at him in a comforting way. He looked at the trees, and he saw the half-closed eyes of the Owl gazing down at him. He glanced to the right, and there sat the Harvest Mouse peeping at him. He glanced to the left, and there was the Mole with its nose poking out of the ground. Around his head flew a Butterfly, and over his toes ran a large Rain-beetle. Only in front of him sat the Fox, waiting for him to speak.

'Well, Tim Rabbit? Well? Anything to say?'

'No, Mr Fox, except there's a lot of my friends all round. They won't let me be hurt,' said Tim.

The Fox looked hastily about him. Every creature was very still. The Owl seemed to fade into the shadows of the leaves. The Harvest Mouse hid behind a blade of grass. The Mole turned to stone. The Butterfly dropped behind Tim's ear and whispered encouraging words to the little Rabbit. The Rain-beetle crept under Tim's toes.

'I see nobody,' said the Fox, uneasily.

'They are all there,' replied Tim. 'They won't let me be hurt.'

The Butterfly flew into the Fox's ear.

'Tally-ho! Tally-ho! The hounds are coming,' she cried.

'Did I hear something?' asked the Fox. He looked behind and went a few steps towards the trees. The Hedgehog rolled after him, and stuck his pins in the Fox's legs.

'What's that pricking me?' cried the Fox.

The Owl flew down and nipped the Fox's body.
'Who's that biting me?' cried the Fox.
The Harvest Mouse pulled the Fox's tail.
'Who's that pulling my tail?' asked the Fox.
The little Rain-beetle tickled the Fox's toes.
'Oh! Oh! Who's tickling my toes?' wailed the Fox.
Now there is one thing a Fox doesn't like and that is to be tickled, especially by a Rain-beetle. So although the Fox didn't much mind the Owl's nip, or the Mouse's tail-pull, or the Hedgehog's prick, he couldn't bear that Rain-beetle tickling his toes. He leapt up, but the Rain-beetle leapt also, fast in the red hair.

'Tally-ho! Tally-ho! Tally-ho!' called the little Butterfly in the Fox's ear.

'Wait a minute, Tim Rabbit. I want you to meet my family, but I've got a terrible tickling in my toe. I'm going off for a bathe. I shan't be long. The stream is just across the glade. Stay here. Don't leave this pile of firewood, Tim.'

'I won't leave the pile of firewood,' promised Tim.

Away went the Fox, galloping across the wood to the stream, and in it he plunged. Away in the opposite direction went Tim Rabbit, pulling the load of firewood behind him.

'I won't leave the firewood. Oh, no,' said Tim, laughing to himself.

'You've been a long time, Tim,' said Mrs Rabbit, when Tim panted up to the door with his load.

'I promised I wouldn't leave the firewood, Mother.'

'Promised who?' asked Mrs Rabbit, puzzled.

'The Fox. He's expecting me to dinner today. He wants his family to meet me.'

'Oh Tim. I'm very glad you didn't go to dinner with him. You would have been the dinner, I fear.'

'Yes. I thought so too, Mother. Have you cooked my apple-dumpling?' asked Tim.

'The biggest dumpling I've ever made,' said Mrs Rabbit. 'I don't think you can eat it all.'

Tim looked at the big apple-dumpling which his mother brought out of the pot.

'Yes. I have room, although I am stuffed with sugar-plums and honey the Fox says,' said he.

X. Tim Rabbit and the Shadow

One sunny day Tim Rabbit was walking on the hillside where the bracken grew. It was like a forest of green trees, cool and shady. He stepped aside and went among the brown hairy stalks, where the air was rich and fragrant, and the ground mossy and soft. Suddenly he stopped, for in front of him, on the short turf lay a little black Somebody. It was curled up in a ball, fast asleep. At least Tim thought it was asleep, but as he tiptoed up to it, the Somebody raised its black head and peeped at Tim with bright eyes, wet with tears.

'Please, sir! Please, sir!' said the Somebody. Tim jumped in surprise to hear the husky, dusky voice.

'Please, sir, I'm lost! Oh dear! Please will you take me with you? I don't like being alone in the world.'

'Who are you?' asked Tim, as the little black Somebody uncurled itself and stood up.

'I'm a lost Shadow,' wept the little person. 'I'm quite lost. I've lost my master and I'm all alone.'

'Whose Shadow are you? Who's your master?' asked Tim, staring at the little black Somebody. He saw a curly head, and a snub nose and twinkling eyes, but it wasn't a rabbit. Oh no, it was like a boy.

'I belong to a boy,' said the Shadow. 'He's ill, and they wouldn't let me go to him. They shut the door on me.'

'Poor little Shadow! I can't help you,' said Tim. 'I've got a rabbit shadow of my own, thank you.'

'Take me with you,' begged the Shadow. 'I'll be good. I'm so lonely, I can't bear it any longer.'

The Shadow sobbed so loudly that even the bees stopped humming, and the jays came peeping down with mocking cries.

'Lost! Lost!' they jeered. 'Not even a rabbit hole to live in.'

It wept such quantities of tears that the ants bathed in the round drops. Crystal clear were the tears, not black as Tim expected.

'Come along,' said Tim, gruffly. 'Stop crying and come with me.'

Mrs Rabbit was very much surprised to see the shadow of a little boy come creeping into her cottage.

'Who's this?' she asked. 'Who is this dusky black man you've brought home?'

'It's a Shadow, lost and lonely, Mother,' said Tim, quickly. 'Let it stop here! It has no mother! No nobody!'

'Poor little Shadow,' said Mrs Rabbit, and she held out her motherly arms. The little black Shadow leaped into them, and clung to her warm furry body.

'Oh! I'm so glad to come here! Don't send me away,' it cried.

Mrs Rabbit was very much surprised to see the shadow of a little boy

'No. We'll keep you,' said Tim and Mrs Rabbit together.

'Though I don't know what your father will say,' said Mrs Rabbit to Tim. 'The house is very small, and your bedroom only holds you.'

'I'll go under the bed,' said the Shadow. 'I'm very thin. I take up no room at all.'

'And then, what about food? We've no rich food for little boys. No chocolates or sugary buns.'

'I don't want anything to eat. I only want company,' said the Shadow, and it leaped from Mrs Rabbit's arms and danced round the table. Tim danced after it, and together they played hide-and-seek.

Mr Rabbit said he was glad the little Shadow-boy hadn't brought a Shadow-gun. It seemed a nice little thing, he said. Quite well-mannered, and polite. When they sat at table the Shadow passed the dishes, and never ate a morsel, although it pretended to eat.

It was almost as good as having a brother for Tim. It was so nimble that nobody could catch it, and sometimes it grew very tall, touching the ceiling and sometimes it shrank to a very tiny size.

Tim was very happy. The Shadow sat at his feet while he had supper, it went to bed with him, and it lay curled up on the mat under the wooden bed. In the mornings it ran outside to the fields with Tim. It helped him to pick mushrooms and blackberries. Even when the sun didn't shine the Shadow was there, waiting for Tim.

It wanted to go to school with the rabbit, but here Tim had to refuse his friend. What would Old Jonathan, the schoolmaster, say if the Shadow of a little boy turned up at lesson-time? So the Shadow stayed outside the circle of blackberry bushes till Tim came out. Then home it ran, holding Tim's paw, and Tim's own rabbit shadow ran by his feet.

'There goes Tim Rabbit with two Shadows,' mocked the Magpies.

'Where did you find that funny two-legged Shadow?' asked the Hedgehog.

'It hasn't any fur,' said the Mole. 'The hair on its head is curly, but there's no fur on its face.'

'Its hind legs are too long,' said a rabbit.

'Its ears are too short,' said another.

'As for its nose!' laughed a third.

'I'll fight you all if you say anything against my Shadow-boy,' cried Tim angrily. He flung his little fists about and cuffed the nearest rabbit. In a minute there was a battle between Tim and a big Jack Rabbit. Tim's own shadow could only bob about at Tim's feet, but the Shadow-boy was free. It sprang on the back of the big bad rabbit and smacked him and nipped him till he ran shrieking away.

'Thank you, Shadow-boy,' said Tim, puffing for breath. 'You know how to fight.'

'My master taught me,' said the Shadow. 'He was the best fighter of all the little boys. Oh dear! Oh dear! I do miss him.' It burst into tears and lay down on the ground.

'I thought you were happy with me,' said Tim reproachfully.

'Yes, dear Tim. It was only that I remembered him,' sighed the Shadow.

One day Tim met the Fox walking in the wood.

Tim dodged into the bushes, but the Shadow didn't follow. Instead it ran up to the tawny Fox and spoke to him.

'Hallo, Mister Fox. Glad to meet you. I know some friends of yours,' said the Shadow.

'Who are you?' stammered the Fox, dodging away

from the dark Shadow-boy and looking around to find the person who cast this strange shadow.

'My master's father has a pack of hounds,' began the Shadow. 'Shall I call the Shadow-hounds, Belle and True and Ringer?'

'Belle and True and Ringer,' whispered the Fox, and like a shadow himself he sidled through the brush-wood and fled.

Little Tim Rabbit came out with a scared face.

'I don't like hounds either,' said he. 'Not a bit. Not a tiny bit.'

'It's all right, Tim. I remembered my old friends,' said the Shadow.

One day Tim and the Shadow started off together, but this time the Shadow led the way. Tim couldn't catch up with it.

'Follow your leader! Follow your leader!' called the Shadow, and it leapt over tree trunks, and across ditches, and over walls. Little Tim hurried and scurried on his short legs, panting after it.

The Shadow led Tim through a little white gate and up a garden path.

'I can't go here,' said Tim. 'It's a house. I'm not allowed here.'

'Stay in the garden, Tim, under the lavender bush,' whispered the Shadow. 'Come here with me. Here.'

So the two of them, and Tim's own little rabbit-shadow, hid in the bushes. They watched the low windows of the thatched cottage. The Shadow gave a thin whistle, only the shadow of a whistle, but at the sound the robin on the rose tree began to sing, the blackbird answered with a trill, and the thrush cried, 'Who's there? Who's there?'

The curtain at the bedroom window moved, a little hand drew it aside, and a little pale face with bright eyes looked out.

The Shadow leapt from Tim's side and waved its black hand. The little boy threw open the window, and gave a shout of joy.

'Shadow! Shadow! Oh, my little Shadow! Come back to me.'

Away sprang the Shadow, away, climbing the rose tree in a flash, and into the room.

Tim could hear laughter and shouts and a great chatter of voices. He hesitated, and lolloped quietly down the path to the gate.

'Hallo, there, Tim Rabbit!' cried somebody, and the little boy and his black Shadow were waving from the window.

'Good-bye,' called Tim.

'Good-bye, Tim Rabbit,' answered the boy, and the Shadow echoed, but its voice was fading away.

Tim ran all the way home. He felt lonely without his old companion.

'I'm glad the Shadow has gone back,' said Mrs Rabbit, when Tim told his story. 'He will comfort that human boy. You can't keep a strange shadow for ever, Tim. Look at all the other shadows waiting for you. Ferns, and birds, and rabbits' shadows all want to play, and they were quiet when that Shadow-boy was here. Now they are ready to play with you again.'

Yes, outside on the common, every little shadow seemed to be swaying and dancing with delight to see Tim with his own little shadow. As for the human boy, he heard many a tale of the world of animals and birds, told to him by his little dark Shadow.

XI. Tim Rabbit's Sneeze

One day it rained and rained without stopping. The streams were swollen to little rivers, and new streams came running down the lanes, tearing up the stones, and sweeping the leaves before them. Pools formed in the hollows, and ponds filled every hole and dimple on the common. Little Tim Rabbit stood at the door of the small cottage watching the bouncing rain.

'Can I go out, Mother?' he asked.

'No, Tim,' said Mrs Rabbit, shaking her head. 'No. You would get wet to your skin.'

'I wish I had a mushroom umbrella,' sighed Tim.

Five minutes later he asked again.

'Can I go fishing, Mother?'

'Certainly not,' said Mrs Rabbit. 'Even the fish have gone into their houses to play.'

'I wish I were a fish,' sighed Tim.

He took a piece of chalk and made some squares on the kitchen floor. Then he played hopscotch, dancing and hopping in and out of the squares, with a stone balanced on his fur toe.

Next he played marbles, and rolled his little clay marbles in the hollows of the floor.

He helped his mother to bake a cake, and he sat on the hearth and sang a song.

At last the rain stopped and the sun began to shine with a watery face. Tim looked out at the wet world. 'Can I go out now, Mother?' he asked.

'Yes, Tim, but keep away from the rain pools,' said Mrs Rabbit.

Tim fetched his fishing-rod from the corner and ran outside. Every little pool and streamlet reflected the sunbeams. The common was all a-glitter. Raindrops shone like gold, and sparkled like fish-scales.

'There must be lots of goldfish there,' thought Tim.

He went across the wet grass, and sat by the edge of a small newly-made pond. It was rippled with little waves, and each wave was tipped with sunlight. At the bottom of the water Tim could see the daisies and buttercups growing. He dipped his hazel rod into the pond and waited for a fish to bite.

> 'Little Tom Fishy,
> Come to my dishy.
> Come to be fried in our frying-pan,'

he called, and the waves flashed and the water laughed at little Tim.

From the bough of an overhanging tree a bird looked down. It spread its feathers to dry them in the sun, and lifted a leg, and winked at Tim.

'Tim Rabbit! Tim Rabbit!' it called. 'You'll never catch a fish that way.'

'Hallo, Magpie,' said Tim, looking into the leafy

branches at the bright eye and the gleaming feathers of the wicked bird.

'The goldfish won't nibble at your bait, Tim. They like something special,' said the Magpie.

'What do they like?' asked Tim.

'Throw away your fishing-rod and dangle your feet in the water. They will nibble your toes,' said the Magpie.

'I shouldn't like that,' said Tim, quickly.

'They have no teeth, Tim. They'll only tickle you. When you feel a sweet tickle, grab the little goldfish from the water.'

'Thank you, Magpie, I never knew that,' said Tim, humbly, and he dangled his little furry toes in the water. For a long time he sat, and the sun went in, and the gold waves became dark. A cloud passed over the sky. Tim's toes were very cold and he shivered, and then he sneezed.

'What are you doing there, sitting in the water, Tim Rabbit?' scolded the Hedgehog.

'Fishing for goldfish,' said Tim.

'There ain't no fish, goldfish or silverfish, in that rain-water pool. Get you home at once, Tim Rabbit, and warm yourself by the fire, or you'll catch a cold.'

Tim climbed out of the water, and he sneezed again. He felt very wet and rather miserable. He ran unsteadily, for his legs were stiff.

'Mercy me, Tim!' cried Mrs Rabbit. 'Where have you been? Your feet are soaking wet, and your nose is blue and your eyes are watering.' She held up her

'Thank you, Magpie, I never knew that,' said Tim

paws in horror. She seized her little son and dried him with a warm towel and rubbed him with hay. Then she put him on a stool near the fire.

'A-tishoo! A-tishoo!' sneezed Tim.

'Deary me,' cried Mrs Rabbit. 'You'll sneeze the roof off. The house isn't as strong as it was. The roof was never mended after that gale in March.'

Tim sneezed again, and the roof of the little house shook.

'I must send that sneeze away or the house will fall down,' cried Mrs Rabbit in alarm.

She made Tim some hot blackcurrant tea, and he sipped it. She poured out a pan of hot water and sprinkled yellow mustard flowers in it. Little Tim sat with his feet in the nice water, and the steam curled round his head, but still he sneezed.

'A-tishoo! A-tishoo!'

There came a knock at the door and the Hare looked in.

'What is the matter, Mrs Rabbit? I heard a very loud A-tishoo come from your house, and I saw the roof-thatch wobble. Is it safe?'

'Little Tim has caught a sneeze,' said Mrs Rabbit.

'Where did you find it, Tim?' asked the Hare.

'I found it out fishing,' said Tim, and his voice was croaky and muffled in the steam.

'Put a fur bandage round your throat,' said the Hare. He pulled some fur from his pocket. It was soft grey fur.

'Oh, thank you. Thank you,' said Mrs Rabbit. 'What a kind Hare you are!'

'I've been young myself, and I know about wet feet,' said the Hare. 'My son, Sam, comes home after fishing and this is how I cure his colds.'

Mrs Rabbit made the delicate fur into a bandage. She wrapped it round little Tim's neck. It was very comfortable and warm, but the tiny hairs tickled Tim's nose, and he sneezed more than ever.

'A-tishoo! A-tishoo!' went Tim.

The house shook, and a bit of the ceiling fell down.

'Oh, dear me!' cried Mrs Rabbit, wringing her paws in dismay. 'I'm sure the house will tumble to bits if I can't stop Tim from sneezing.'

She put him to bed, in the corner of the kitchen by the fire, but still he sneezed.

There came another knock at the door.

Tap tap! Tap tap! A squirrel peeped in.

'Whatever is the matter, Mrs Rabbit? Such loud A-tishoos come from your house, my oak tree rustles. Is there anything wrong?'

'Oh, Miss Squirrel!' cried Mrs Rabbit, wiping her eyes on her apron. 'Tim has caught a sneeze. He can't get rid of it. I'm afraid it will blow the roof off. What shall I do?'

'Give him a dose of dandelion syrup, sweetened with honey,' said the Squirrel. 'I always take it when I have a cold.'

She put her paw in her bag and brought out a root of dandelion and a honeycomb.

'Oh, thank you! Thank you, Miss Squirrel!' said Mrs Rabbit. 'What a kind Squirrel you are!'

She made the dandelion syrup, and gave Tim a

spoonful. It was very soothing to his throat, but he sneezed again.

'A-tishoo! A-tishoo!' he went, and the picture of 'Snow-White' fell from the wall with a clatter.

'Oh, deary me,' cried Mrs Rabbit. 'Our best picture broken. The house will never stand the strain of this.'

She patted Tim and muffled him up, and put a log on the fire.

There came a tiny tap on the door. It was such a little tap it could hardly be heard, Tim was sneezing so loudly.

A Hen walked in, with little beak uplifted and wings fluttering anxiously.

'What is the matter, Mrs Rabbit?' she clucked. 'I was walking your way with my husband the Cock for company and I heard the A-tishoos. Is anything wrong?'

'Oh, Mrs Hen,' sighed Mrs Rabbit. 'My Tim has caught a sneeze, and he cannot get rid of it. I'm afraid it will blow our house down. What shall I do?'

'Give him an egg well beaten, and mixed with a pinch of poppy-dust,' said the Hen. 'I always take poppy-dust for a cold.'

She laid a brown egg on the floor, there and then.

'Oh, thank you! Thank you!' cried Mrs Rabbit. She broke the egg in a bowl and beat it to a froth with a twig and dropped a pinch of poppy-dust into it. Then she gave it to Tim.

'A-tishoo! A-tishoo!' he went, and the roof moved and shook.

He only sneezed the more.

There came a gentle push at the door and a Cow mooed softly outside.

'Whatever is the matter, Mrs Rabbit?' she lowed. 'The cattle are troubled by the loud A-tishoos coming from your cottage. Can I help you?'

'Oh, Mrs Cow. Mrs Mooley-Cow,' cried Mrs Rabbit. 'My little Tim has caught a sneeze, and we cannot get rid of it. What shall I do?'

'Give him a mug of warm milk,' said the Cow. She stood still by the door while Mrs Rabbit milked her into a bowl.

'Oh, thank you! Thank you, Mrs Cow,' said the Rabbit. 'What a kind Cow you are!'

She poured the warm frothy milk into Tim's own china mug, and held it out to Tim. He drank and he drank. He smiled happily, for he felt much better. Then suddenly he sneezed again.

'A-tishoo.'

It was such a loud sneeze that everybody and everything seemed to listen.

Tap! Tap-tap! Tap-tap-tap! Who was that at the door? Mrs Rabbit looked at Tim and Tim looked at Mrs Rabbit.

'Who's there?' called Mrs Rabbit.

Tap! Tap-tap! Tap-tap-tap!

The tip of a long red nose and white teeth came through the little door. It was the Fox himself.

'What is the matter, Mrs Rabbit?' he asked, in his

smooth oily voice. 'I can get no peace for the loud
A-tishoos that come from your house.'

'Oh, Mr Fox,' stammered Mrs Rabbit, and she was
all of a tremble with fright. 'My little Tim has caught
a sneeze, and it won't go. I'm very sorry, sir. I don't
want to trouble you, sir. I'm afraid it will blow my

roof off, and we shall have no home. What shall I do,
sir?'

'Let me in, Mrs Rabbit. I'm a first-class doctor. I can
cure any rabbit of a cold. Open the door very wide, so
that I can get in.'

'Oh, no, Mr Fox,' said Mrs Rabbit, and she looked at Tim. Tim shook his head.

'I want to feel his pulse, poor Tim Rabbit,' said the Fox in a wheedling tone. 'I will drive that sneeze away.'

'Oh, no, Mr Fox,' said Mrs Rabbit stoutly. 'You might eat us, pulse and all. Oh, no, thank you. I would rather have the sneeze than the cure.'

'Just as you like, Mrs Rabbit. Keep your sneeze. I won't help you.' The Fox snorted angrily and went away.

Little Tim Rabbit sat up in bed, and his eyes were bright. He was so frightened that he quite forgot to sneeze. Then away out of the chimney flew that sneeze, and the house stopped shaking and the roof settled comfortably again on the timbers.

Little Tim Rabbit cuddled close to his mother and in a minute he was fast asleep. In the morning the cold had quite gone.

As for the sneeze, it climbed to the top of the fir tree, and there it lives, A-tishooing when the wind blows hard. You can hear it if you listen on a cold winter's night when you are safe in bed.

XII. Tim Rabbit's Party

Such a rubbing and a scrubbing was going on under the ground, in the little cottage where Tim Rabbit lived! Such a dusting and a cleaning and a polishing of the candle-sticks and the pepper-pot and saucepans! Mrs Rabbit's kitchen was shining with all the little bright things you can imagine.

Little brass mirrors hung on the wall, copper pans were ranged on the shelf round the room. In small hollows were glow-worms, shining with their own green light. Hanging from the ceiling were bunches of rosemary and thyme and lavender, sending out sweet smells. The ground was covered with a new carpet of wild flowers, tiny blue and white blossoms with petals like silk.

Mr Rabbit was walking up and down giving the final touches. Mrs Rabbit was cooking the buns and cakes, piling them on dishes. Tim was darting in and out, carrying jugs of spring water, for lemonade and ginger-beer, although of course it wasn't ordinary lemonade and ginger-beer. No, the lemonade was made of honey and rose leaves with a pinch of lemon balm, and the ginger-beer was made of the hot flowers of snapdragon and dandelion.

Whatever was all this excitement for? It was Tim Rabbit's birthday and he was having his first real party. All his school friends were coming. Old Jonathan had given them a holiday. Seven little school mates would be there, all except one belonging to the famous family of Rabbit – Adam and Bill Rabbit from Nettle Lane, Charlie and Don from Tansy Common, Fanny and Kate from Daisy Dell, and last of all, little Sam Hare.

'Wherever shall we put them all?' asked Mrs Rabbit. 'There won't be room to sit down!'

'We don't want to sit,' said Tim, quickly.

'I mean your father and me to sit down,' said Mrs Rabbit. 'We shall want to rest our old bones.'

'Oh, I shan't be here,' said Mr Rabbit quietly. 'I can't stand the clatter of all that crowd. I shall go out to the woodshed to do a bit of carpentry.'

'Well, Father. I shall be sorry to miss you, but you would be rather in the way,' said Tim, politely.

'Hum,' grunted Mr Rabbit, rather crossly. 'I shall make a rabbit hutch if you're not careful, Tim.'

'Cakes, sandwiches, buns, pasties,' said Mrs Rabbit, running to the table from the pantry and putting out the plates of good things. 'Wild thyme buns, and saffron buns. Sage cheeses and crab-apple pasty. Egg and sorrel sandwiches. Dandelion slices. All fit for the King of England himself, bless him.'

'Cherry jam and sloe jam. Hawthorn jelly and rose-hip jelly,' said little Tim, dancing round the table, and looking at the white pots, each with a wooden spoon at its side, and a cap of green leaf covering it.

Mrs Rabbit was cooking the buns and cakes

Mr Rabbit opened the door of the medicine cupboard in the wall. 'Wormwood tea, rue tea, bittersweet mixture, castor oil and weasel-snout ointment. That's what you will want if you eat all this,' said he, and his eyes twinkled at little Tim.

'We haven't any lettuces,' cried Tim suddenly. 'I'm going to get some. I know where they grow. In Aunt Eliza's garden.'

'It isn't safe there, Tim. Aunt Eliza seldom goes in her garden. There's a new gardener, a very spry young man.'

'I don't care a pin for the new gardener,' said Tim, throwing back his head proudly.

'Now Tim! Don't boast. We have enough without lettuces. Go out and gather a bunch of flowers for the centre of the table. Be quick. They are coming at three o'clock.'

Tim ran off, but he had made up his mind to get the lettuce.

'Lettuce?' said Aunt Eliza, when Tim knocked at her door and scampered in to the little house by the garden. 'There's a new gardener, not like the old, deaf, sleepy one. I haven't been since he came. I was warned!'

'I don't care a pin for the new gardener,' said Tim. It's for my birthday party, Aunt Eliza.'

'Well! Well! I'll find a birthday present for you, and be quick back, Tim. Don't dawdle or he may catch you.'

Tim went through the hole in the wall, that was

Aunt Eliza's private doorway. Oh dear! He was caught in a net spread across the opening. He dashed right into it, and it wrapped itself round him. He was frightened, poor little Tim! He could hear the gardener digging in the distance, and the birds singing in the trees over his head.

'Poor Tim Rabbit! Caught at last!' they sang.

'There's nobody to set him free!' called the Woodpigeons.

'What shall we do?' asked the Thrush. 'What shall we do?'

'Let him go! Let him go!' cooed a Dove.

'You'll catch it! You'll catch it!' mocked the Magpies.

Everybody seemed to be talking and giving advice to poor little Tim Rabbit, who lay there in the net.

The gardener looked at the birds, listened a moment, and stuck his fork in the ground.

'Something going on to make those birds chatter,' said he, and he strode across the vegetable beds.

'So, I've cotched you, young varmint,' said he, and he lifted Tim up by the ears and looked at him closely.

'Please, sir – please, sir –' stuttered Tim.

'What was ye after? Eh?' asked the gardener.

'A lettuce for my birthday party,' stammered Tim. It was difficult to speak with one's ears held up.

'A lettuce? A birthday party?' said the gardener, and he scratched his head, but he didn't let Tim go.

'Yes, sir,' said Tim, faintly.

'Are ye any relation of Tim Rabbit?' asked the gardener, and he actually smiled at Tim.

'I am Tim Rabbit, sir. I am Tim. I am him. I am Tim. I am,' said Tim quickly.

'Then if so be ye are that selfsame Rabbit, I've a mind to –'

'What?' asked Tim, as the man hesitated.

'To take ye home with me. For my own children have heard of ye. They'll want to see ye. They told me to keep my eyes open for a bunny in a blue coat.'

'Please, sir, if you'll let me go, I'll tell your children a tale. Yes, I will,' cried Tim.

'Nay, I'll take ye home first,' said the gardener. He stuffed Tim in his pocket, but Tim gave a leap and out he jumped. Away across the garden he scuttered and the gardener ran after him.

'Can't stop!' cried Tim, squeezing under the gate. 'I shall be late for my party.'

The gardener laughed and threw a lettuce over the garden wall.

'Take your lettuce, Tim Rabbit, and mind ye come to my cottage one night soon and tell a tale to my little ones.'

'I won't forget,' promised Tim. He picked up the lettuce and ran back to Aunt Eliza.

'Oh, Tim, I thought you was cotched,' she cried.

'Yes. I was, but he let me go,' answered Tim. 'Have you got my present, Aunt Eliza?'

'Here it is, Tim.' Aunt Eliza held out a bit of looking-glass she had found in the wood. Tim could see his nose and his whiskers in it. It was a really wonderful present, and Tim hugged his Aunt Eliza as he thanked her.

Then away he ran home. The guests were already straggling along the paths, one behind another. Six little rabbits and Sam Hare dawdling along at the end. Tim dashed through the bushes and got home first.

'They're coming! They'll be here in a minute,' he cried, and he washed his dirty hands and brushed his hair before his own looking-glass just in time.

The company came up to the door. Pit! pat! they came. They tapped and giggled, and shuffled on their soft feet, and whispered as they rapped on the door.

When Mrs Rabbit opened to them, they crowded in, filling the room, and Mr Rabbit sidled out of the back door.

'We've brought you some presents, Tim. Many happy returns of the day,' they said, and they held out their gifts.

A string-bag, but of course it wasn't made of string, but of horsehair, from Adam Rabbit.

A piece of honeycomb from the wild bees' nest, from Bill.

A book made of nut leaves sewn together, but there was no printing in it, from Charlie.

A ball, not made of rubber, but of cowslips, from Don.

A purse, not made of leather, but of puffball skin, from Fanny.

A set of ninepins, but they were really fir cones, from Kate.

A lovely red pincushion, but it was a robin's pincushion from a rose bush, from Sam Hare.

'Thank you! Thank you! Thank you!' cried Tim with delight as he took the presents from his friends.

First of all they had tea, and they ate everything up, so that the plates were quite clean at the end of the feast.

Then they played games, for the table was moved away into the field to make more room. They played postman's knock. Each one tapped at the little green door just like a real postman, but of course they brought rabbit-kisses in their bags, not real kisses. You know what rabbit-kisses are, don't you? Rabbits rub their little soft noses when they kiss.

They played musical chairs, but they had no chairs, for Mrs Rabbit was sitting on the only one. The music came from a wheat-stalk pipe, that she played to keep them running.

They danced, but their dance wasn't a waltz or even a polka. It was a Bunny-trot, which is quite fun to dance. There was no band, but a nightingale and a thrush and a blackbird in the little wood close to the door sang their sweetest for the company.

They pulled crackers, but they were not the crackers you know, made of coloured paper and tinsel with a bang and a toy inside. The crackers were the long seed-cases of the balsam, that go off like a fairy gun when anyone touches them. They had great fun with these.

They rang hand-bells and played a tune, but the bells were not those you play. They were harebells from the fields.

They played hide the thimble, and even that was different, for Mrs Rabbit's thimble was a foxglove flower which she put on her paw when she did the mending.

All the time they played they could hear a little tap, tap, tap, going on outside in the woodshed.

'What's that noise? Is it a woodpecker?' asked little Adam Rabbit.

They danced a Bunny-trot

'It's Father doing his carpentry,' said Tim. 'He likes tapping.'

So on they went, and they made such a racket that even the tap-tap of Mr Rabbit's hammer could hardly be heard.

They said good-bye and went off down the garden path, calling 'Good-bye' and 'Thank you very much,' but still the tap-tapping went on.

'They've all gone now and it's been a lovely party,' called Tim at the keyhole. 'Come out, Father.'

'I can't! I've been hammering all this time to tell you I'm fastened in,' cried Mr Rabbit, and his voice sounded very cross indeed. 'Why didn't you come before?'

'We thought you were working, Father,' stammered Tim. He shook the door and ran in to the kitchen to call his mother.

'Father's stuck!' he cried. 'He can't get out.'

Mrs Rabbit pulled, Mr Rabbit banged with his hammer. The little door of the woodshed was fast as if it had been glued.

'It's locked, and the key's gone,' said Mrs Rabbit.

'Somebody's gone and fastened you in, Father,' shouted Tim.

'I know that. I guessed as much two hours ago,' grunted Mr Rabbit. 'I'm hungry and here I'm stuck.'

'Who can have done it?' whispered Tim to his mother.

In his heart he knew. It was little Sam Hare, of course. Sam didn't care a brass button for anybody.

Sam had gone out of the room for postman's knock, and when they called he came in with a sly look on his face.

'Who can have done it?' whispered Mrs Rabbit to Tim.

'Never mind who done it or who didn't done it, it's done and I'm nearly done,' groaned poor Mr Rabbit, whose hearing was sharper than they had imagined.

So Tim and Mrs Rabbit pushed and banged, and Mr Rabbit hammered and stamped, but the little door was made of sturdy oak, and what could three little rabbits with their soft paws and a small hammer do? The woodshed was far older and stronger than the house they lived in.

'Somebody's got the key,' said Mrs Rabbit.

'Of course they have,' shouted Mr Rabbit. 'You would have unlocked it if the key was there, wouldn't you?'

'Don't shout, my dear,' said Mrs Rabbit. 'The neighbours will think we are quarrelling, and we never quarrel.'

'We shall quarrel now if I don't get out,' roared Mr Rabbit. 'I'm hungry.'

'We can feed you through the keyhole,' said Tim, hopefully.

'I won't be fed through the keyhole,' shouted Mr Rabbit.

'You can only pour soup through a keyhole, Tim,' said Mrs Rabbit sadly.

'I don't like soup,' roared Mr Rabbit.

'I'll go and look for a key,' said Tim.

He brought the key of the cuckoo-clock, and the key of the money-box, but they wouldn't open the door. He brought the wooden spoon and the silver salt spoon, but they wouldn't unlock the door.

'I'll find Sam Hare and give him what for, locking up my father,' said Tim to himself.

'I'll go and look for the key, Mother,' he said aloud. 'I 'specks it's somewhere about.'

Out in the ploughed field little Sam Hare was leaping and dancing with delight. He was singing a ditty, and the words came faintly to Tim as he raced towards his friend.

> 'One, two, three.
>   I found a little key.
>   I put it in a wooden box,
>   And hid it in a tree.

> 'One, two, three.
>   I've lost my little key.
>   I threw it down a dark hole,
>   And now it's hid from me.'

'Where's that key, Sam? You took it. What have you done with it?' shouted Tim.

'I've lost it. Can't 'member where I threw it,' said Sam, and he turned head over heels. He was madly dancing in the wind.

'My dad's as cross as two sticks,' remarked Tim.

'Is he?' Sam was surprised. 'I thought he would laugh.'

'He's hungry. He wants to come out,' said Tim, solemnly.

'I never thought of that. I'll try to find it, Tim.'

Together they ran in and out of the trees, looking for a hole. It is astonishing what a number of holes and hiding-places there are in a wood. Every tree has a cupboard where a Hare may hide a tiny iron key.

'It's like hunt the thimble,' said Sam Hare. There

was a scutter of feet and the rest of the party came to join them. Eight little animals, all hunted here and there in the wood, and at last there was a shout of joy. Little Adam Rabbit found the key, shut in its walnut-shell box, put tidily in a hole in the beech tree's roots.

When Tim got home he found poor Mrs Rabbit fast asleep on the doormat, and Mr Rabbit's snores came from the woodshed.

Tim unlocked the door and awoke his father.

'Is that you, Tim?' yawned Mr Rabbit. 'Did you find the key?'

'Yes, Father. It was in a beech tree,' said Tim demurely.

'Very strange. Very strange that the key of our woodshed should get in a tree,' said Mr Rabbit, as he walked out of his prison.

'There are strange things in the world,' said Mrs Rabbit. 'I'm glad we have No Ordinary Rabbit to find our lost key.'

Tim coughed and blushed. They went indoors and soon Mr Rabbit was eating his hot posset, and hearing all about the party.

'I promised to go to the gardener's cottage and tell a tale to his children,' said Tim.

'Tell them about me being locked up by little Sam Hare,' said Mr Rabbit.

'How did you know?' cried Tim.

'That would be telling,' said Mr Rabbit softly, and that was all they could get out of him.

So the next night Tim went to the cottage and sat outside the window. He told his tale to the gardener's little children, but what he said must wait for another time.

Other Young Puffins by Alison Uttley

Magic in My Pocket
Little Red Fox
More Little Red Fox Stories
The Little Knife Who Did All the Work
Fairy Tales by Alison Uttley *chosen
  by Kathleen Lines*
Stories for Christmas *chosen by
  Kathleen Lines*
Adventures of Sam Pig
Sam Pig Goes to the Seaside
Sam Pig Goes to Market
Sam Pig and Sally
Yours Ever, Sam Pig
Sam Pig at the Circus

and for older readers:

The Country Child
A Traveller in Time